OTHER

Harlequin Romances

by ELIZABETH HOY

Many of these titles are available at your local bookseller,
or through the Harlequin Reader Service.

For a free catalogue listing all available Harlequin Romances,
send your name and address to:

HARLEQUIN READER SERVICE,
M.P.O. Box 707, Niagara Falls, N.Y. 14302
Canadian address: Stratford, Ontario, Canada.

or use order coupon at back of book.

THAT
ISLAND SUMMER

by

ELIZABETH HOY

HARLEQUIN BOOKS   TORONTO
WINNIPEG

Original hard cover edition published in 1973
by Mills & Boon Limited, 17-19 Foley Street,
London W1A 1DR, England

© Elizabeth Hoy 1973

SBN 373-01695-6

Harlequin edition published June 1973

Printed in Canada

CHAPTER ONE

JENNIE came out of the house into the early morning sunshine with an outsize shopping basket slung over her arm. More pannier than basket; it folded flat because it was made of dried palm fronds, closely woven. The house behind her was pink-washed and plainly designed, looking what it was, a comfortable and unpretentious family house. It was called the Villa Planina to indicate that it stood on a high hill, '*planina*' being Serbo-Croat for 'mountain'. A spacious terrace ran along the front of it, stone-paved and dotted about with tubs and urns full of brightly coloured flowers—pink and scarlet geraniums, purple zinnias and bright red salvia. An assortment of well used wicker garden furniture showed that much of the life of the household was conducted out here. Wide curving stone steps led down to an overgrown garden, beyond which lay the wooded hillside that descended to the port of Modice below, capital of the island of Zelen—Green Island, truly named for its wealth of trees and flowers.

Crossing the terrace to the rear courtyard where the family cars were garaged, Jennie halted to look down at the scene which never failed to delight her with its beauty; a coastline of wooded cliffs and little bays with sandy beaches, golden in the morning's golden light. The sky was an arc of pure blue, the windless air sweet with the perfume of dew-wet roses and the more subtle scent of the thyme and rosemary which covered the rough hillside. Jennie breathed it in deeply.

How she loved it all! This remote Adriatic island on which her family had spent the summer months of every year as long as she could remember. Undiscovered by tourists or holidaymakers, it had provided a sanctuary for Jennie's father, the celebrated painter, Adrian Romaine. Here he could escape from unwanted publicity

. . . the gossip columnists, reporters and newshawks who dogged his footsteps. Lately it had been publishers' agents as well, since it had got out about that he was writing his memoirs. He wasn't, as it happened, he would have hated the labour involved, but the rumour circulated and nothing would scotch it. Perhaps because he was of an age to be writing memoirs, old enough to be Jennie's grandfather rather than her father, though young enough in heart to be almost her contemporary. She was the youngest of his six children, and the most beloved, the older ones having scattered and married, most of them with children of their own. Twice widowed, Adrian had married as his third wife Karla Burnett, who was something of a celebrity in her own right, being a novelist of distinction. At the moment she was away from home, lecturing in the States to culture-hungry American women's clubs. So Jennie in her mother's absence had her adored father to herself, and was enjoying her role as chatelaine of his household.

Doing the day's marketing was one of her regular chores, gathering from the open-air stalls on the quay-side at Modice the fruit and fresh vegetables Marie, their elderly French cook-housekeeper, would need for the day's meals. She had been in the family's service most of her life, and when she wasn't with them on Zelen looked after the Left Bank apartment and studio Adrian used on his occasional visits to Paris, though his headquarters, as befitted a famous British artist, were in a tall old house which stood behind a screen of trees and garden on the Chelsea Embankment. Marie enjoyed her summers on Zelen and never complained no matter how many guests there were, and Adrian, incurably sociable and hospitable, did not spare her. At the moment the household included Jennie's half-sister, Claire, with her French film director husband, Jacques Lemaître, and their three-year-old daughter Dympna, inevitably known as 'Dimples'. There was Dimples' nannie too, of course, a young relative of Marie's from Brittany named Lucille—and a sad, thin, way-out litte sculptor of uncertain age from Montmartre—Jean Duprès, whose message to the world was expressed in lumps of old scrap iron and coils of twisted wire. At least that was how Jennie had seen his efforts when she visited one of his Paris exhibitions on the art-famous Rue de la Seine.

Poor Jean, he looked as if he never had enough to eat, and probably didn't; which would be one of the reasons large-hearted Adrian had invited him to stay at the villa for an indefinite period.

To wind up the party there was Gervase Lemaître, Jacques' young brother, aged eighteen and wildly in love with Jennie—who didn't reciprocate. Not that she didn't like Gervase and enjoy being with him, but at her ripe age of twenty he seemed hopelessly immature. And in any case her heart had long ago been given to John Davenham, the son of Sir Mark Davenham, the distinguished Harley Street physician who had been Adrian Romaine's doctor for half his lifetime. John, his only son, was following in his steps and was now approaching the final stages of his hospital training. Jennie had adored him since she was nine and he fourteen. It was during a shared family holiday here on Zelen three years ago that they had spoken of their love to one another—but there was no formal engagement and indeed at that stage no talk of marriage. Jennie was still at finishing school, John walking the hospital and bogged down with study. So that they met only at holiday times and then briefly, but their contacts were lit with a romantic glow. It had seemed to Jennie a wholly satisfying state of affairs. She did not look ahead. The future, vaguely and deliciously exciting on the far horizon, could take care of itself.

She was not thinking of that future now, nor of John, as she edged the big Cortina out of the garage and through the courtyard gateway into a narrow road which had not long since been a mule track. Roads and cars were a fairly recent innovation on the island of Zelen. This one wandered crazily, first turning inland to climb a stony slope and then suddenly twisting in its tracks to plunge down to Modice and its busy harbour.

As Jennie swung the car round the last bend of the

way she could see the twice-weekly steamer from the mainland heading for its berthing place. Long and white, and elegant, it was the island's only contact with the Dalmatian coast towns. There was no air-strip on Zelen, no planes could reach it, for which Adrian Romaine thanked heaven. The visits of the steamer were stirring events, the days of the week marked by them. Tuesday and Friday were invariably referred to as Steamer Days. So that the week went: Monday, Steamer Day, Wednesday, Thursday, Steamer Day.

Jennie's eyes widened now as she looked down at the approaching ship. Gold-flecked hazel eyes, set in a sensitive heart-shaped face. A week hence, next Tuesday, when the steamer came in it would be bringing John, arriving to spend a well-earned holiday with the last of his current exams out of the way. A quick sense of anticipation warmed her as she parked the car and made her way to the cluster of stalls which were grouped under the walls of the ornate Town Hall, once the mansion of some wealthy Venetian merchant during the days of the island's subjugation to Venice. It was very lovely in its baroque fashion, its façade decorated with carved stone cupids trailing long festoons of carved flowers and leaves. On either side of the Town Hall there were houses of equal beauty—a beauty born of blood and conquest. Zelen had paid dearly for her exquisitely designed little capital city, crowned by its miniature cathedral, which stood on a high plateau above the harbour, its twin campaniles delicately outlined against the tender morning sky. Jennie seldom looked at it without a stab of sheer joy at its loveliness. But busy now finding what the stalls had to offer, she was not thinking about the cathedral.

Figs, peaches, the little woodland strawberries, and more mundane but equally mouth-watering, the piles of scarlet tomatoes, creamy cauliflowers, bunches of asparagus, purple aubergines and avocados, baskets of young green peas and slender beans: lettuces too, she mustn't forget them. Marie in her Parisian way insisted upon serving a plain green salad with every meal.

The pannier was half filled, leaving room for the lobsters and gigot Marie had ordered, when the steamer's siren rent the air. Jennie turned to watch it coming to rest at its usual berthing place, propellors noisily churning the water, sailors on the high deck shouting and throwing ropes to the stevedores who waited on the quayside to catch them and tie them around the great fat bollards placed at intervals along the quay.

Moving towards the quay's edge, drawn by the general excitement, Jennie wished she could have seen John's tousled tow-blond head among the crowd of passengers waiting to disembark. Supposing, she thought improbably, he had managed to get away a week earlier than he had anticipated! But of course that was impossible. It was during the next few days that he would be sitting for his final medical exam. So there could be no John today.

Later she was to wonder how it would have affected the strange events of the coming week if he *had* arrived that golden summer morning. Perhaps the strange events would never have happened. But much, much later, looking back over those June days on Zelen, she was to decide that it was destiny rather than chance which shaped all that was to come. At the moment, however, there was nothing to warn her that this morning was different from any other morning when she had lingered over her marketing to watch the steamer tie up.

Suitcases and baggage of all kinds were now being flung lightheartedly over the ship's side to land on the quay—passenger luggage, mostly. The stevedores, dark-eyed Slavs and round-faced Croats, ignored it, concentrating on the more important mail bags, tea chests, agricultural implements, and the hundred and one incidentals fed to the island from the mainland.

The passengers now beginning to come down the gangway looked about them curiously. It was easy to pick out the English holidaymakers being met by a uniformed porter from the Slavonia, the first luxury hotel to be built on Zelen, an innovation the significance of which had hardly yet dawned on the island's inhabitants. Only Jennie eyed these arrivals with vague misgivings, until her attention was caught by a dark-haired man standing alone on the deck, obviously keeping clear of the tourists' rush to land, although he was to all appearances as English as any of them. But with a special English arrogance, lacking in the jostling hoi-polloi. He was tall, broad-shouldered, with lots of untidy dark hair, and he was looking straight down at Jennie in a purposeful way which made her feel slightly embarrassed. In the moments immediately following she couldn't help watching him. With an air of assurance he came down the gangway, cleared at last of the chattering tourists. He snapped his fingers at a loitering stevedore, who ignored the summons.

"Are there no porters about?" the stranger demanded of no one in particular in a tone of disgust. He pointed, in case anyone was interested, to the muddle of suitcases on the ground, his own, no doubt, among them. "Porter!" he called, and once more was ignored, perhaps because he had spoken in English.

"Try it in Italian or German," Jennie found herself advising on a wholly unexpected impulse. She wasn't in the habit of offering advice to strange men. But this particular incident seemed to demand her intervention—as a matter of simple politeness. Stepping on to Yugo-Slav territory for the first time can, for the uninitiated, be a confusing experience. Europe is suddenly left behind, or so it seems; the air is faintly oriental, with a hint of Iron Curtain, although the brand of National Socialism is far from the rigidity of orthodox Communism, and the Serbo-Croat people are incurable individualists—an independence born of their incredible resistance to centuries of foreign invasion. They are not hewers of wood and drawers of water, nor do they meekly trot across the quay laden like donkeys with baggage of chance travellers. Arrivals carried their own luggage on Zelen, or its transport was arranged for them by Putnik, the local travel agents. Most of the current suitcases were now being picked up by hotel servants from the Slavonia.

Whether some of this dawned on the dark-haired man

or not Jennie couldn't know, but the slight shrug of his broad shoulders was eloquent of resignation. Turning, he smiled at her, his rather hard face softening. His eyes, once more fixed on her with the odd intentness they had held when he had looked at her from the deck, were a clear very dark blue, thick lashes emphasising them, giving a touch of femininity to the essentially masculine features.

"I don't think I'll bother with a porter," he said. "I can easily carry my one suitcase myself. It's just that I was hoping some local character might materialise who would be able to recommend an inn where I could put up."

"You aren't booked in at the Slavonia, then?" Jennie asked, somewhat unnecessarily.

He shook his head. "That sort of international caravanserai I avoid when I can. I'd rather stay somewhere I can get close to the people of the island." He patted a breast pocket. "I've even bought a Serbo-Croatian phrase book to help me with my efforts to speak the lingo. It's a relief to know that I may be able to get by with Italian or German, though I'm not very strong on either. But it will be better than tangling with the formidable consonants of the Serbo-Croat tongue."

Jennie laughed. "They aren't so bad as they look in print. Not that I find them all that easy..." She hesitated, realising that this rather odd conversation had gone on long enough, and the dark blue eyes fixed on her had an unaccountably disturbing effect. Like all pretty girls of twenty she was accustomed to interested male glances, but there was something more than interest on the face of the man confronting her—a sort of questioning appeal.

"Are you on holiday here?" he was asking, when a steel-bound crate, swinging on a carelessly manipulated crane, came perilously close and grazed Jennie's shoulder, knocking her off balance. Only the stranger's promptness in catching her saved her from falling into the harbour basin.

For a moment she rested against him, feeling stunned

and dizzy. Her shoulder hurt and she had dropped her shopping basket. The world swayed about her ... she was afraid she was going to faint.

"Sit down here a moment." The young man edged her gently towards a roomy bollard. Gratefully she sank down on to its sun-warmed surface.

"Are you badly hurt?" He was probing her shoulder with a gentle fingertip. She winced.

"I don't think anything is broken," she told him, raising her arm experimentally. "It's just a hefty bruise."

"Clumsy oaf!" the stranger growled, anathematising the operator of the derrick and crane, who, unaware that anything untoward had happened, had deposited the steel-bound crate on to the quay and was winding the crane back into the ship's hold. Nobody seemed to have noticed the small mishap—the bustle of arrival still seethed, the package tourists now being shepherded into a waiting coach, with 'Hotel Slavonia' painted in gold lettering along its side. Donkey carts were being loaded with lesser items of freight. A couple of business-like lorries waited to collect the agricultural machinery, and there was an official-looking mail van to pick up the mail bags.

"How about going across to that café over the way so that you can sort yourself out?" the stranger was suggesting. "You look as if you could do with a strong coffee."

When he put out a hand to help her to get up off the bollard she placed her own into it without hesitation. She still felt ridiculously shaken and the thought of a cup of coffee was irresistible.

"If you'd just wait a tick until I have retrieved my suitcase," the young man said, making for the depleted jumble of luggage on the cobblestones.

They set off across the cobbled pavé, the young man carrying Jennie's shopping pannier as well as his own case. Beginning to be inwardly amused at her bizarre little adventure, she stole a glance at his lean and shapely profile. What had brought him all on his own to this out-of-the-way island? Apprehension stirred. Was he some wandering newspaperman? Or worse still a purposeful publisher's agent who had decided to risk a confrontation with the elusive Romaine in his summer hiding place?

"They can get at me for six months of the year in my city pads," Adrian would say. "But for the other six months I'm guarding my privacy, and God help the journalist or literary tout who disturbs it."

The café, with a flourishing 'Kafana' spelled out in Cyrillic lettering across the door's lintel, was empty and cool, its small windows shuttered from the blinding morning light. Whitewashed walls, a red-tiled floor, plain scrubbed wooden tables, a zinc-covered bar counter, suggested a pleasing simplicity.

"It's a bit rough and ready, I'm afraid," the young man offered apologetically as they sat down at one of the tables.

"It's all right," Jennie assured him, glad to be resting in the shadowy coolness. Her shoulder was aching badly. She wished she could slip her frock down and examine the damage—but in the circumstances that was hardly possible!

"Will my sketchy Italian get us by in here?" her companion was wondering, when the cheerful, swarthy-looking man behind the bar greeted them with a hearty, "*Dobro jutro!*—Good morning. *Is volite, Gospodin, Gospodja?* What can I do for you, sir and madam?"

"*Kafa, molim vas,*" Jennie answered him valiantly.

The swarthy man smiled at her Serbo-Croatian effort. "You are English," he pronounced triumphantly, speaking in that tongue. "Londoners perhaps? I suspected it the moment you came through the door."

"So much for my Serbo-Croat accent!" Jennie said.

"And for what I hoped was my cosmopolitan appearance," the young man added. "I might as well have arrived with a bowler hat and rolled umbrella."

"The typical London City gent," the bartender put in unexpectedly, and seeing their surprise threw back his head and laughed. "You wonder what I have to do with London city gents, eh?" And without waiting for an answer he went on : "You wouldn't think it, no? But for several years I worked in London at a five-star restaurant called the Golden Tower—in Soho. Do you know it?"

"Do I know it !" the young man echoed. "It's been a haunt of mine when I'm entertaining, or being entertained, for more years than I care to remember."

Delighted by the coincidence, the barman came from behind his counter and stood by their table. "I was a waiter on the balcony floor. Is it possible that I may have had the honour of serving you there, sir?"

"Highly possible," the young man agreed.

"Then more than ever may I welcome you to my *kafana* and to Zelen." The barman held out his hand. "Nikole Sisak," he presented himself.

"Glyn Harney," the stranger responded, taking the proffered hand and shaking it.

"And your good lady?" queried the irrepressible barman. Jennie blushed and was furious with herself for her embarrassment.

"Alas no," returned Glyn Harney gallantly. "We've only just met on the quayside. The young lady was struck on the shoulder by a swinging crane and she's bruised and shaken. I've brought her in here for a reviving drink of some kind. Coffee, or perhaps . . ." he indicated the shelves of bottles behind the counter, "something stronger."

"You are hurt, *Gospodja*?" Nikole asked in horror.

"Not very badly," Jennie assured him. But when she touched her shoulder she winced.

Nikole made commiserating noises. "My wife is in the kitchen," he volunteered, nodding towards a baize doorway behind the bar. "If you will permit I will take you to her and she will find some salve for your hurt."

Jennie was glad to go with him, and even more glad that he did not seem to have recognised her as the daughter of the distinguished summer resident Adrian Romaine. All this polite introducing and handshaking might have led to an awkward situation. Though she hadn't thought about it until this moment it was all-important to keep her identity from Glyn Harney, at least until she was sure he wasn't a predatory journalist.

In the kitchen, smelling of woodsmoke and garlic and ripe cheeses, Gospodja Sisak, a plump middle-aged woman with hard rosy cheeks like two shining apples, was full of concern for the young English lady who had been hurt by the careless crane-driver. Her English was not quite so fluent as her husband's, but she coped valiantly and with Jennie's few words of Serbo-Croat the situation was soon under control. Nikole had returned to the café, so that Jennie felt free to display her naked shoulder, revealing a purple and scarlet bruise. Mrs Sisak, with exclamations of horror at the injury, produced a jar of home-made ointment which smelled of the island's thyme and rosemary. When she had gently massaged it into the bruised shoulder she covered it with a comfortable bandage. Feeling better already, the pain subsiding under the influence of the soothing remedies, Jennie thanked Mrs Sisak and rejoined the men.

Cups of scalding Turkish coffee now stood on the wooden table, flanked by small glasses of the fiery plum brandy known as slivovitch. This with the thick sweet coffee was the universal breakfast drink in Yugo-Slavia, Jennie explained to Glyn Harney, who obviously thought a bowl of café au lait would have been more suitable for her.

"Do you mean to tell me that you drink this fire-water first thing every morning?" he marvelled, as she swallowed the plum brandy at one gulp. She shook her head, laughing, her eyes watering from the pungency of the brandy.

"No, of course I don't. Actually I dislike slivovitch, unless as an after-dinner drink, but I felt I needed a bit of a booster this morning after my set-to with that wandering crate."

"How is the shoulder now?" Glyn Harney enquired anxiously.

It was much better, she told him, and having finished

her coffee pushed her cup aside with a dismissive air, saying she must be on her way.

"Don't go yet!" he urged with an odd urgency. "Stay and hear my good news. Mr Sisak is going to give me a room and board here, which happily ends my search for accommodation."

Nikole Sisak spread his hands in a deferential gesture. "The gentleman has not yet seen the room I am offering him, but I assure him it is comfortable; large and bright overlooking our garden at the back. I will put a table in it, to make a desk at which he can work."

"At my writing," Glyn Harney explained to Jennie. "I've just been telling Mr Sisak I hope to do a survey of Zelen, its history, its background, its people, its beauty. That's why I've come here. Actually I'm doing a series of island surveys; I've already done Cyprus, the Greek Islands, Corsica, Sardinia."

A writer, Jennie thought with a qualm. But what sort of a writer? Would his survey of Zelen include the winkling out of Adrian Romaine in his jealously guarded hideout? "You're a historian?" she hazarded.

"Not exactly a historian, nothing so distinguished, I'm afraid. My little treatise, indeed the entire series, is designed for a non-academic public and must have popular appeal. Zelen, the green island, ought to go down well. As the steamer approached it this morning it seemed to me an enchanted place—so small, so lovely, the tiny walled city with its golden campaniles rising above the rose-coloured cliffs and jade green sea. The perfume of its gardens came out to meet us. A subtle perfume I couldn't quite place."

"Rosemary and thyme," Jennie supplied. "It grows in the scrub all along the cliff top. The scent of it's everywhere."

"Sweet as the singing of Ariel in *The Tempest*, drawing the shipwrecked Ferdinand to the shores of Shakespeare's magic island," Glyn Harney said. "Where he found his Miranda," he added softly, with a glance which made Jennie feel self-conscious and foolishly disturbed. Just what was he up to, this arrogant young man with his romantic literary allusions? His scrutiny embarrassed her—as if he were sizing her up. And if so, what was he making of her? Turning away from him, she encountered her reflection in a small clouded mirror which hung on the wall beside the table. There she was with the tangle of bronze-gold hair she had brushed too hurriedly before leaving home. Nor had she stopped to put on any make-up—not that she ever wore much, but her shiny nose would have been the better for a dab of foundation cream. Her heart-shaped face, lit by eager hazel eyes under dark level brows, looked too young, too vulnerable. Though that was not quite how she saw it herself. She only wished she had been a bit more well-groomed. In heaven's name why? To impress this unknown Glyn Harney? Though he had been kind to her because of her hurt, he could not possibly care whether she was well groomed or not. Nor did she care—about his not caring.

"I really must go," she exclaimed with an oddly hunted air. "I still have some marketing to do." She gathered the laden straw pannier up from the floor.

"Marketing?" Glyn Harney eyed the basket of fruit and vegetables. "You're not just a summer visitor, then . . . you live here?"

Caution kept her silent a moment, then she said guardedly, "I'm staying at a villa up on the hill."

"With friends?"

His questions were beginning to border on the impertinent. She left the last one significantly unanswered, saying once more that she must go. "Thank you for the coffee and slivovitch . . . and for coming to my rescue on the quayside."

"I hope the shoulder is really better," he offered in a tone of warm concern. "Do you think you should see a doctor about it?"

She shook a lock of her unbound hair out of her eyes. "Oh, no, that will be quite unnecessary. The pain has almost gone. Mrs Sisak's remedies have helped a lot." And anyway, she could have added, I'll have my own doctor with me next week. John Davenham, almost

M.D., with the thatch of bright hair and the kind grey eyes. In so short a time he would be with her. The thought brought a strange sense of comfort and safety— a refuge into which she could run. Though run from what? She slung her shopping basket over her arm. "Thank you once more . . ."

"You really have to go?" Why must he make such a thing about it? she thought impatiently.

"And you haven't told me your name yet," he probed.

"It's not important," she returned nervously, and was startled to see the swift shadow of disappointment which clouded his glance at this curt dismissal.

Standing to take his leave of her he seemed to tower over her. "I gave you mine," he reminded her. "I hoped our introductions might be mutal."

Romaine. She wasn't going to give it to him—a name that resounded with fame throughout more than one continent. This Harney man who talked like a poet and dined at the Golden Tower, rendezvous of London's cultured élite, would be sure to pounce on it. Let him find it out if he had to in his island investigations. But she wasn't going to help him to threaten her father's privacy.

"I'm Jennie," she told the stranger.

"Just Jennie?" he echoed, with a reproachful lift of an eyebrow.

"Just Jennie," she repeated.

He held out his hand and she put her own into it. His clasp was firm and strong and lasted longer than was strictly necessary. Nor did she like the tingle in her nerves his touch engendered.

"Shall I be seeing you again, Just Jennie?"

She shook her head. "I don't think it's very likely."

Withdrawing her hand from his, she turned to the bar counter where Nikole Sisak had been effacing himself tactfully washing glasses. "Goodbye, *Gospodin*," she took leave of him. "And please thank your wife for being so kind about my shoulder."

He gave her a little formal bow. "It is a pleasure for us to have served so beautiful a young lady!"

The Serbo-Croatian fulsomeness did not embarrass her. She smiled at the kindly Nikole and avoiding a final glance at the standing Glyn Harney, went out into the sunshine. It was as if the morning in all its beauty came running to meet her, the blue-green sea dancing, sparkling with an almost unbearable brilliance. She had to shield her eyes from it. The cries of the still labouring stevedores were like a wild, gay chorus.

Emptying the heaviest part of her load into the boot of the car, she went up the steep flight of stone steps which led to the upper part of the town to buy the meat and lobsters. Here was the little cathedral, surrounded by a network of ancient narrow streets where every house had its own individual colour and design. There were the small dark shops too, selling hand-made lace, the great silver brooches and pendants of a kind the women of the island had worn for generations. There were holy ikons too and slender wooden flutes carved by the shepherds to while away their hours of watching over their flocks in the rough far away hills. But the dominant feature was the cathedral with its slender twin spires topped by the golden crucifixes, the insignia of the island faith.

Even in her preoccupation with lobster and lamb Jennie was vividly aware of the beauty all about her. She would never tire of this plateau high above the rosy cliffs of Zelen; the tree-lined square where velvet-eared donkeys awaited their owners in welcome patches of shade, heads patiently bowed, tails switching against the assaults of stinging flies. Women in colourful national dress, like characters on some operatic stage, called to one another as they went about their business. The knife man in flamboyant velvet coat and scarlet neckerchief sharpened the housewives' knives on his whirring wheel. It was all part of the day's lighthearted mood, a joyful drama in which she was playing a part. But just what part? Leaning over the low parapet which enclosed the south side of the square, she looked down the rose-coloured cliffs to the date palms and cacti and flowering shrubs below, and beyond them a tumble of golden and amber rocks with the sea lapping gently against them.

An enchanted island, the stranger had said. Why had he spoken of Ferdinand and Miranda—that rather obscure pair of Shakespeare lovers? And how had their story gone—told in *The Tempest*? Rather boringly, from what Jennie remembered, recalling dull sessions in the English class at school. But Glyn Harney hadn't made them sound boring. Lovers on a magic island.

Lobsters! she thought, with a pang of duties forgotten, and went on her way, her heart singing.

CHAPTER TWO

BACK at the villa Jennie carried her purchases into the kitchen where Marie pounced on them with the enthusiasm the true Frenchwoman never fails to show towards food. "Monsieur is already breakfasting on the terrace," she announced. "I will bring you your *café crême* when you join him. There are some fresh croissants in the oven. . . ."

"Sounds mouth-watering!" Jennie exclaimed. The Turkish coffee and brandy hadn't taken the edge off her appetite. She went out on to the terrace where her father hailed her with delight. When he was not in his big garden studio, painting, he hated being alone. Human company and plenty of it was the breath of life to Adrian Romaine. And Jennie's company was specially precious. She was the child of his ageing years, and there had always been a unique bond between them. His eyes were bright with love as he looked at her across the breakfast table; the fresh young face, innocent of make-up, the warm golden-bronze hair, now loosely tied at the nape of her neck; such a young and vulnerable neck, so touchingly slender. He noticed the way her long lashes made small shadows on her delicately modelled cheekbones. She had the sort of bone structure which never failed to delight his artist's eye.

"Why it's only you and I who get up to breakfast these glorious summer mornings I can't think," he said. "There's Claire and Jacques lazing over a breakfast tray in their room, old Jean sleeping off last night's attack on my best claret, and even young Gervase still presumably snoring his head off—since there's no sound yet from the attic of his everlasting transistor pop music. At his age I would have been swimming in the bay long ago."

"At least we have Dimples," Jennie remarked, as the

23

little girl came racing along the terrace towards them, her chubby arms held out.

"Grampy, Grampy!" she called. "Dimples want piggyback. Now. *Now*!" Her voice rose imperiously, and she was tugging at the old man's sleeve, her small face crimson with determination. In the background her young nannie, Lucille, stood looking helpless and abashed. Miss Dimples was impossible to control. There was nothing she could do about it, and for some reason madam the child's mother didn't seem to mind.

"Piggyback!" shrieked Dimples.

The old man, surrendering, leaving his unfinished breakfast, stood up and lifted the very solid little girl on to his shoulders, then patiently set off to trot with her round the garden. Jennie watched them with a twinge of annoyance. Dimples was a darling, but so spoiled that for peace's sake everyone gave in to her.

"More! More!" she yelled when presently Adrian returned to the terrace with his burden.

"More piggyback, Grampy. *More*!"

But there were limits. Breathless and looking oddly grey, Adrian disentangled himself from his small granddaughter and handed her over to Lucille, who led her away screaming blue murder.

"Claire and her theories!" Jennie sighed.

"Never permit a child of three years old to suffer frustration," Adrian quoted bitterly. "To thwart them at this stage in their development is to do them permanent psychological damage. That's what she told me yesterday. Where in heaven's name does she get these ideas?"

Jennie shrugged. "From the latest pundits. The three-year-old, it seems, is going through what's called the 'negative period'. So you must never contradict them. All the contradicting is to be done by the child."

"And Claire swallows this nonsense!" Adrian wiped his exhausted brow, his words still coming out breathlessly. "Doesn't she realise that in another couple of years the fashion will have changed and an entirely fresh set of baby-raising theories will have been thought up by the experts? Meanwhile poor little Dimples is being utterly spoiled."

"It's such a shame," Jennie agreed. "She can be such a little angel when she likes."

"Oh, well," Adrian dismissed the matter, "I expect she'll come out of it all right. Most of us have to survive or adjust to the mistakes made by our well-meaning parents." The glance resting on his daughter sharpened. "Is that a bandage on your upper arm?" he asked in a startled tone.

She put a hand to her shoulder. "It's nothing really." She told him of her misadventure on the quayside and how she had gone into a nearby *kafana* to recover, finding an English-speaking proprietor and his wife who had given her first aid. "I had some hot coffee and a snifter of plum brandy and was none the worse."

"What a clumsy crane-driver!" Adrian said indignantly. "He ought to be reported to the steamship company or the harbour master, or whoever it is that employs him."

"Oh, no," Jennie put in quickly. "Don't let's make a fuss. It's hardly bruised at all, and the crane-driver wasn't even aware that the box he was unloading had grazed me."

"Might have been serious," Adrian growled.

Jennie bit into her second croissant and let the matter drop. Better not mention Glyn Harney—the wandering historian or whatever he was. With luck her father would never know he was on the island. The thought of unaccountable strangers worried him more and more as he got older, specially if they had any kind of connection with the world of books and publishing. In a way it was those damned memoirs lurking at the back of his mind. He felt he ought to have stab at them but didn't know how to make a start. A life as varied and colourful as his was worth recording. But the thought bored him intolerably. The past was the past. He was too busy living in the present to be interested in it. That was what he had told the publishers who had already approached him.

Not that Glyn Harney was a publisher, Jennie reflected. But you never knew. Book writing was book writing and one thing led to another. Glyn Harney must be avoided, ignored. She had told him it was unlikely they would meet again . . . and that was the way it had to be. In some curious way the decision was a relief.

She saw the postman coming up the drive, bringing the letters which had arrived with the steamer. Would there be one from John? He hardly ever missed the twice weekly post, but since he was arriving so soon he might not have bothered this time. She waited while her father and the postman exchanged greetings and gossip. Their morning chats on mail days were an established custom. Very often indeed old Ivan was invited to sit down and have a cup of coffee. Adrian Romaine with his love for people had no sense of class-consciousness. Basically he respected his fellow men and it wouldn't have occurred to him to regard them as anything but equals. The only human beings he despised were the ex-ploiters, the parasites, amongst whom he, somewhat high-handedly, included all gossip writers and what he called 'tattling journalists'.

When at last Ivan had departed in a great gust of laughter at some untranslatable Serbo-Croatian joke, Adrian picked up the pile of letters waiting on the table. With maddening deliberation he began to go through them.

"Isn't that one for me?" Jennie put in impatiently, recognising the familiar blue envelope with John's generously flowing handwriting scrawled over it.

Producing it at last, saying, "Ah, one from the beloved!" Adrian handed it over. His glance was a little wry as he watched the eagerness with which it was received. "He means a lot to you, that young man of yours, doesn't he?" he asked. There was a wistful note in his voice, but Jennie did not hear it, nor did she answer her father's question, only wondering at the bulk of the letter in her hand. It felt as if it contained pages and pages. Why should John write so much when he would be with her in a few days? Faint apprehension stirred as she took the letter up to her room. She liked to be alone when she was reading John's letters and her bedroom was her favourite sanctuary. Here she was safe from the comings and goings of family and guests. It was a pleasant room with french windows opening on to a small balcony, separated by a few feet from the main balcony which ran along the width of the house, above the terrace.

Her bed, still tumbled after the night, was as she had left it when she hurried off to market. Later she would make it herself. She enjoyed keeping her room and the possessions it contained in order, leaving only the heavier cleaning for the island girls who came and went in a rather erratic fashion to help Marie keep the big house ship-shape.

Now, sitting in a lounge chair by the open window, she gazed at the letter in her lap, postponing the opening of it. Dear John! His letters made her feel warm, and wanted. Though it was not as if she were really desolate for love. If her mother had often been an absentee figure, largely engrossed with her own affairs most of the time Jennie was growing up, her father had made up for it. His unwavering devotion wrapped her around, was part of the very air she breathed. He made her feel safe and secure. And so did John. Every word he wrote assured her of his devotion.

"Darling Jennie," he had begun in his last letter, "If only you knew how constantly you are in my thoughts. I keep your beautiful photograph on my study desk—it helps me to press on and on at the endless drudge of swotting for my exams, reminding me that it's for you, my love, I'm working, and for the time when we shall be together for always. . . ."

A time unspecified in an undefined future . . . safely distant.

Opening the blue envelope, she smoothed out the folded pages. "My darling," she read, "Things have been happening thick and fast since I wrote to you last week. I've almost finished my exams and I think I've done fairly well in them. If so my medical degree is in the bag

27

and I can ease off for a bit, enjoy my forthcoming holiday. I can't begin to tell you how much I'm looking forward to it, nor how I long to see you. I know there are still some years of hard work ahead if I'm to become a consultant and join my father in his practice—which is what he and I both want. I have, as you know, always felt it would be wise to complete all this before we thought about marriage. But now I feel I can't bear to wait. I've talked it over with my father and he agrees with me that there's no real need for us to postpone our marriage any longer. That is if you can put up with a husband who has to put in rather a lot of time at his books, in addition to the hours of hospital duty?

"When I tell you the miracle which has just happened I think you'll feel with me that fate is working for us. The tenants who occupy the flat above the Harley Street offices are leaving! And my father has offered the flat to us. Think of it, Jennie—a home of our own. But there it is; ours for the taking. So what about it, Jennie darling? We could be married almost at once, though you would probably prefer to wait until you come back to Chelsea in the autumn, by which time your mother will have returned from her American tour. Anyway, my love, we can talk it all over when I arrive on Zelen next week . . ."

Jennie could read no more. The letter dropped from her grasp and she gazed into space, her eyes wide and incredulous. The moment she had thought of as a distant possibility was upon her. John wanted to marry her almost right away. The few weeks which separated her from the autumn return to London would go by in a flash. By late September or early October she would be Mrs John Davenham. Why should the prospect fill her with panic? Although she had known all along that she and John would marry, she hadn't really faced up to all that it would mean. Well, it was high time she did. Resolutely she picked up the letter and read on. There was a long description of the Harley Street flat. It sounded super. "It's not a bit flat-like in the modern sense," John wrote. "On two levels, with a quaint little staircase leading to the mansard bedrooms which have picturesque mullioned windows. There's a practical kitchen with all mod. cons, a lounge and a small dining room which opens on to a miniature roof garden. Oh, Jennie, it's all too marvellous. I can just imagine us there ... together. It seems almost too much happiness to bear!"

She waited for the answering rush of joy in her own heart—but nothing happened. She just felt flat ... and frightened. Perhaps that was natural. She must give herself time to adjust—get used to the idea of being John's wife. Perhaps it would have come easier if they had been formally engaged. But their relationship had been quite casual, a drifting on from a boy and girl friendship. John had been part of the background of her life ... like the house in Chelsea, the summers on Zelen, the members of her own family. Now, suddenly, he wasn't in the background any more, but very much in the foreground, a dominating figure threatening to alter the familiar pattern. No longer would she be her father's constant companion ... in the Chelsea home, or on Zelen. She would be living in a Harley Street flat with mullioned windows and a practical kitchen where, presumably, she would organise meals for John, and on occasion, his friends. Mrs John Davenham, hostess, housekeeper ... wife.

Going over to the dressing table, she creamed her face and wiped it with a tissue, then applied a little foundation, working through the familiar routine absently. In the mirror her reflection made her look oddly pale under the fall of her bright hair. Her hand shook as she put on a touch of lipstick, and even her lips weren't quite steady. What on earth was the matter with her? Impatiently she pulled herself together. Nothing between herself and John had really changed—merely speeded up a little. Hadn't she believed in their love for one another ever since she was nine years old?

With a resolute air she went downstairs. Claire and Jacques were at the table on the terrace, reading their mail, Dympna beside them in one of her more angelic

29

moods, eating grapes which her father was peeling for her. Jennie joined the little party and helped herself to a peach from the great dish of fruit which was an invariable centrepiece on this family table. She had left John's letter upstairs in her dressing table drawer. Her instinct was to say nothing about it for the moment. Anyway, Claire and Jacques were too interested in their own letters to be easily interrupted, discussing them together in the half-finished sentences husbands and wives often employ—as if words between them were not wholly necessary.

Would she get to be like that with John? And how and when should she make the dramatic announcement! "John and I are going to be married in the autumn." Even hearing the words in her mind gave her a bit of a shock. But she would have to say them aloud sooner or later. The first person, of course, who ought to hear them was her father, who was already away in his studio at the far end of the garden busy with his great and latest work—a study of Zelen's exquisite little cathedral.

Gervase appeared, carrot-haired, golden-eyed and sleepy. He gave Jennie a languishing look as he sat down opposite her. Marie, who kept an experienced ear to the ground for the comings and goings of the family, came out of the house with his coffee and croissants.

Presently they would all bundle into the largest of the two rather ramshackle family cars and go off to their special secret bathing beach the far side of the island. Far away from any possible intrusion from the few tourists and holidaymakers who mostly stayed around the private beach belonging to the Slavonia.

The day took on its usual pattern; the hours of swimming and sunbathing, drowsing at intervals on the hot sandy shore with the thyme-scented cliffs enclosing it. Gervase of course had brought not only his snorkel and flippers but his transistor. When he was not persuading Jennie to have a go at underwater swimming, which she disliked, he was lying by her side twiddling knobs, conjuring up disc-jockey voices from various parts of Europe.

The universal wailings of 'Love, love, love' poured out, the yearnings that never got anywhere, the mournings which revelled in mourning.

"Do we always have to listen to that dismal cater-wauling?" Jacques would ask with an air of strained resignation. Not that he could talk, Gervase reminded him, addicted as he was to his twangy guitar. It was all the usual easy-going family bickering, Claire putting in an occasional peace-making word, a buxom, golden-skinned young goddess, lying in the hot sunshine with her head on her husband's shoulder. How familiarly and naturally their bodies touched. Jennie looked away from them with a sharp unexpected pain. What was marriage really like? Was it in the end the sleepy, good-tempered and somehow passionless contact of Claire and Jacques lying side by side on the big shared striped towel? Or was that just a part of it? Day and night companionship. Never to quite belong to oneself any more. A tremor ran through her—half longing, half fear.

They were late getting back to the villa for lunch, but Marie did not object. Lunch in the erratic household was a moveable feast—cold dishes easily served, salads, fruit, eggs, cold meats. She would see that they ate more adequately in the evening. But it would never be a wholly orderly household. The comfortable rooms were seldom subjected to a major 'turn-out'. Adrian would have hated it if they had been. Life for him had to be free, apparently disorganised. The disciplines he followed had nothing to do with material values. And old Marie who understood him perhaps even better than his brilliant youngish wife was content that it should be so.

Jennie too liked it the way it was. In their Chelsea home under the influence of her mother there was at least a semblance of conventional conformity, but during the blissful summer months on Zelen everyone did more or less as they pleased. Would she still have her long Zelen holidays after she had married John? Jennie wondered that morning, and hastily thrust the question away from her.

*   *   *

31

After lunch everyone slept. Then Jennie and her father went for a walk, climbing the bare stony hill behind the house. It was strenuous going and they did not talk very much, saving their breath for their climbing. If Adrian stopped more often than usual to rest, Jennie did not notice it, absorbed with her own thoughts. John's letter had not yet been mentioned and as the afternoon wore on her impulse to keep silent about it became a formulated plan. After all, there was no hurry about breaking the news. She had a whole week before John arrived. There was no need yet to face the family excitement which would engulf her as soon as she told them all what was in the wind. Time enough, she assured herself. The longer she kept silent the more accustomed she would have become to the prospect of the whole startling upheaval.

So that it was a day like any other Zelen day, save for the secret she carried in her heart. It was late when she went to bed after an evening listening to Jacques' guitar and Adrian's long-playing records on the lamplit terrace, an impromptu concert which ended with a Mozart piano concerto, cool as the dew falling on the thirsty garden, pure as the song of the nightingale who competed from the top of a nearby acacia tree.

In bed at last, Jennie slept the profound sleep of the young, and woke with a start the following morning to find it was well past seven. She would have to hurry down to the quay if she was to get the best of the day's fruit and vegetables. As she flung on the few garments needed that warm sunny morning she was conscious that her heart was beating a little faster than the moment warranted, and if there was an odd eagerness in all her movements she wouldn't admit it to herself. The Glyn Harney man. There would be no possibility of running into him on the quayside at this early hour ... nor did she want to.

Making her way from stall to stall half an hour later in the market place, she was careful to keep her glance .... and her thoughts ... away from the *kafana* the far side of the harbour. She looked at the empty berthing place of the mainland steamer, and tried to imagine what it would be like next Tuesday when John arrived. But the mental picture was oddly blurred and unconvincing. Then, turning her back on the dancing sparkle of the sea, she mounted the long flight of uneven stone steps to the higher reaches of the town. Resting at the top, she leaned on the parapet overlooking the cliff. Now she could see the kafana far beneath her, with its garden spread out behind it—quite a well tended garden, with a path leading down to the footway which led to the shore. Was Glyn Harney already at the table Nikole Sisak had prepared for him, working at his history? It was hardly likely. He would have to collect his material first. What kind of material? she wondered. If he kept to the ancient Venetian conquest of Zelen he would be no threat to her father's peace. Uninterested in contemporary events, he might not even discover that Adrian Romaine was staying on the island. With an unaccountable sigh she let her glance wander out over the vastness of the sea. Smooth and clear this morning, it shone with a rainbow brilliance, its colours ranging from blue to green to amethyst. Small motionless cotton wool clouds hung in a cerulean sky.

"Beautiful, isn't it?" said a voice at her elbow.

Her heart seemed to pitch forward in her breast as she turned to find Glyn Harney leaning over the wall beside her. Her quickly indrawn breath was an audible gasp.

"Did I scare you?" Glyn Harney asked. "I'm sorry."

"I didn't hear you approach," Jennie faltered.

Turning to rest his back against the wall, his hands in his pockets, he surveyed her. His steady glance held a twinkle of amusement, which vaguely annoyed her.

"Are you always so jumpy?" he asked. "Or is it a hangover from yesterday's accident? How *is* the shoulder?"

"Practically okay," she told him. "How is the *kafana*?"

"Oh, fine. The house is much larger than one would expect from the quayside approach. I've got a sizeable first floor room overlooking a garden which leads right

33

down to a small enclosed beach, so that I can practically step out of bed into the sea for my early morning swim. The bed in my room, by the way, is quite the largest I've ever seen, like the baron's bed of medieval times. An entire family could sleep in it."

Jennie nodded. "And probably have done. That's how Yugo-Slav beds are in country places." For some obscure reason her cheeks were growing warm as she spoke. What on earth was the matter with her ... stuttering and stammering and turning colour just because Glyn Harney had come upon her unexpectedly and was now talking about ... beds.

"You've already been in the sea," she noticed, her glance going to the dark hair which was still wet.

"I was swimming soon after six," he told her. "And since seven I've been haunting the market stalls on the quay, hoping I would see you. But you were later this morning. When you didn't turn up I decided to console myself by coming up here to have a look at the cathedral."

His words fell on her with an almost physical impact. But he was talking nonsense, of course, chatting her up in a rather too obvious fashion. It was all a little cheap. She turned away from his dismissively, picking up her basket. "Good morning, Mr Harney. I still have some shopping to do." Her intention was to sweep away, leaving him crushed and crestfallen. But instead he had firmly taken hold of the big pannier and was saying, "This is much too heavy for you. Let me be your porter until you've finished your shopping—and then perhaps we could have a cup of coffee."

Ignoring the suggestion, she put out her hand, trying to get the pannier away from him, saying in an agitated tone : "I can quite well carry this myself." And then as she tugged in vain at the straw handles : "Do you always thrust yourself upon people you scarcely know in this mannerless way, Mr Harney?"

"No, Just-Jennie, I don't," he answered, unabashed. "And you're not someone I scarcely know; you're *you*— unique and beautiful, a face lifted up to greet me as the

34

steamer came to berth yesterday morning. You seemed to me to be a part of the island's enchantment. That sweep of aquamarine sea, curving in and out of wooded bays; the little town with its rose coloured walls, the cathedral's twin spires high against the sky . . . it was all breathtaking. And there you were with your shining hair and exquisite face, lovely and unspoilt as the first hours of the summer morning."

She did not speak when he fell silent, her heart halted by the bizarre turn the conversation had taken, so poetic an outpouring that it was almost impersonal, like clear chords of music. She had dropped her hands to her sides, leaving him in possession of the basket. Oddly, she was no longer angry with him, no longer on the defensive.

It was the stranger now who seemed ill at ease; his urgent glance conveying pleading . . . apology.

"I know I must sound utterly mad to you," he said, "but please have mercy on my madness. Let me talk to you a little while."

"I don't think you're mad," she answered. "Just a bit foolishly sentimental, if you don't mind my saying so." She had to play it down— not let herself be affected by the strange things he had said to her, or the intense way he was looking at her. "The island is extraordinarily lovely and people approaching it from the sea are apt to get worked up by it. But you must not confuse your reaction with me."

"Unfortunately I already have," he said. Somehow, as if by common consent, they were walking along the cobbled way which led away from the tree-shaded square and the shops towards the cathedral. She did not resist him any more; a strange feeling of inevitability pervaded her.

"And you won't yet tell me your full name," he went on. "But that somehow adds to the magic. You're a film star perhaps, hiding from unwanted publicity?"

She laughed and shook her head. "Nothing so interesting." If only he knew how near the publicity bit came to the truth!

"Then you're a princess, travelling incognito. Or perhaps you're not flesh and blood at all, but a lovely illusion. A princess-ghost, wandering out of the pages of this troubled little island's chequered history."

"I'll settle for being the ghost," she told him.

He did not smile. "Dear Just-Jennie!" he said. They had reached the limit of the cobbled way now, its ending blocked by the façade of the cathedral. Wide leather doors, inches thick and reinforced with iron hinges, hung open. Air cool and fragrant with incense flowed out of the marble interior to meet them. They passed under the sculptured lintel and stood on the threshold of the holy place. Rose and white marble walls soared to the elegantly vaulted roof. The main aisle was broken by pointed arches which led to a high altar of lavish magnificence over which hung an immense golden baldachino. The whole effect was one of perfect harmony—radiating an air of peace.

"Only love could have built this place," Glyn Harney said at last, softly. "And here it stands intact, after a thousand years, unmoved by the barbaric assaults of Romans, Turks, Venetians. . . ."

So he had done his homework, Jennie thought, was already familiar with the cathedral's history.

They wandered round the aisles, lingering while Glyn Harney pointed out garlanded coats of arms, the canopied pulpit, the exquisite carving of the handful of choir stalls.

"You're gathering material for your book," Jennie suggested. "You seem to know quite a lot about Zelen already. Your book when it's written should be full of learned information."

He shook his head. "Not learned," he said. "If you mean it in the academic sense. I'm committed to keeping it light enough for a not very learned public, like the booklets which have appeared after my other island surveys. They're really glorified travel talks." He shot her a surprisingly diffident glance. "You're never come across any of them, I suppose."

"No, I'm afraid I haven't," Jennie admitted, feeling

inadequate. Travel talks. There was her cue, she was to realise later . . . if she had had the wit to seize on it. But she was too absorbed with the strange turmoil of her feelings to be quick on the uptake. Here she was walking and talking with the man she had determined to avoid, and she didn't know quite how it had come about, nor what there was about him which seemed to make their companionship inevitable. Because it *was* a companionship. With every moment they spent together she felt more and more at ease with him. It seemed quite natural that she should be sharing his delight in the architectural beauties around them, and even more natural that he was carrying the heavy basket of fruit and vegetables.

They were standing now before the high altar, looking up into the dome of tender blue which covered it. "If we can get a shot of this at this angle. . . ." he was musing aloud. And then turning to her he explained that a photographer would be joining him later. Even then she didn't suspect the real nature of his activities. Books, even booklets, she assumed carelessly, would be the better for a few illustrations.

When at last there was no more to be noted and they were leaving the building Jennie held out her hand for the shopping basket. "You mustn't let me keep you," she said dismissively. "I've enjoyed looking at our little cathedral through your knowledgeable eyes, but now I must get on with my marketing."

He swung the basket out of her reach. "But you said I could be your porter until you'd made all your purchases," he reminded her.

"*You* said it; I didn't," Jennie corrected severely.

"Does it matter who said it?" His grin was disarming, his darkly blue eyes flashing with mischief. Ruthless eyes in their way. Magnetically they held her glance. He was exciting, this man. There was a sense of power about him. He was so disturbingly sure of himself, refusing defeat even in so small a matter as the carrying of a shopping basket.

She made no further attempts to get it from him,

37

recognising that he was too much for her. He had way-laid her intentionally this morning and he would make of their meeting just what he intended. She ought to be angry with him, but she was not, her pulses beating unevenly. Never before had she met anyone quite like Glyn Harney.

While she shopped he effaced himself, but coming down the steps to the quay a little later he remarked on the extent of her purchases. "You must be a large family," he suggested.

"We are," she agreed, and added sternly, "Don't probe!"

"I won't," he conceded. "I like your incognito act. It's intriguing . . . as long as it doesn't mean I must never see you."

"I can't promise anything," she told him.

"The island can be a lonely place," he sighed.

"Then why didn't you book in at the Slavonia? You would have found plenty of company there."

"The Slavonia is hardly the background that appeals to me—a great concrete caravanserai filled with holiday-makers. Last night they played dance music until well past midnight. I could hear it distantly from my room in the *kafana*. It might have been coming from the Blackpool Tower—just the usual modern garish caco-phony. What I was hoping to hear, while I'm on the island, was Yugo-Slav music. And I would like to see some of their beautiful traditional round dances."

"Such as the *kolo*," Jennie suggested. "You'll find that sort of thing more in the inland villages than on the coast. There's a place called Urbino about ten miles over the hills. . . ." She broke off, halted by the urgency of his glance.

"Take me there," he demanded.

She drew in a swift breath.

"Please!" he begged. "I'm afraid I'm not being very tactful or polite about this, rushing it at you. But this is immensely important to me; it would be of the greatest value to me to have someone like yourself to show me

38

the ropes . . . a knowledgeable guide. I've got the impression that you're pretty well at home on Zelen."

A remark she ignored as she said quickly that the dancing at Urbino didn't usually start until pretty late. "It wouldn't be easy for me to get away. . . ."

"I see. Well, if it's quite impossible . . . I realise I'm asking rather a lot. Only, as I've already said, it is rather important to me."

His humility disarmed her. And she could see his point. A section on folk music and folk dancing would be essential for his book. He could go to Urbino alone, of course—but why shouldn't she accompany him, supplying snippets of information he might miss on his own? But that wasn't the whole of it. She wanted to go with him, she admitted to herself. It would be fun to sit with him outside the inn at Urbino, watching the young men and women whirling through the intricate figures of their dance to the music of native fiddles. A scene that would surely help him to catch the romantic atmosphere of Zelen as nothing else would.

"I'm perfectly respectable, if that's what's worrying you," she heard him say. "The Kingfisher Press, who publish my books, would vouch for me."

A well-known educational publishing firm. It sounded all right. But it had never occurred to her that he was anything else but conveniently acceptable. She told him so, adding with a laugh, "You reek of respectability with all your architectural knowledge about cathedrals. It isn't that which makes me hesitate. . . ."

"What, then?"

Their glances held and she felt her heartbeats quicken. I want to come with you so much that it frightens me. The words flashed through her mind, but they were far too revolutionary to be uttered aloud, or even inwardly acknowledged. A wild and incredible notion to be suppressed before it had time to take root. It was in a purely impersonal way that this man interested her, she told herself. She liked his appreciation of the island and the way he had talked about the little cathedral. Architectural beauty was important to him and he enjoyed sharing it. It was, she persuaded herself, because he was so keen on his island survey and because she felt she might be able to help him a little that she found herself saying, "Tonight, then, if you like I'll drive you to Urbino. I could pick you up with the car outside the *kafana*. After dinner . . . about nine o'clock."

"But this is wonderful!" The way his face lit up made him appear younger than she had thought.

"A night of traditional Yugo-Slav dancing . . . what a chapter for my book!"

A remark which, while it assured her, at the same time obscurely disappointed her. His work of course meant everything to him, which was as it should be. She held out her hand for the controversial shopping basket. "I really must hurry home now."

"No time for coffee this morning?"

She shook her head. "Thank you, but no."

"I shall see you this evening, then."

They had reached the quayside and he walked to the car with her, watching her as she drove away.

"*A bientôt!*" she heard him call after her exultantly, as she turned the car.

"*A bientôt,*" she whispered under her breath. To our happy meeting!

CHAPTER THREE

SHE drove up the hill to the villa at a reckless speed—running away from her thoughts. What on earth had made her agree to take this unknown young man out to Urbino? A wild promise given on an unaccountable impulse. But she would keep her promise... meet Glyn Harney on the quayside this evening as they had arranged. And after that? It wasn't a very long drive to Urbino, the village in the hills. Claire and Jacques had discovered it several years ago and since then it had become an occasional rendezvous for the members of the Romaine family and their guests. They had become quite friendly with Stefano, the proprietor of the one and only inn. Supposing he addressed her by her name this evening, Jennie thought with an uneasy pang. But it wasn't very likely. He mostly addressed her casually as '*Gospodica*', the Serbo-Croat equivalent of 'Miss'.

Anyway, she couldn't go on hiding her identity from Harney indefinitely. As long as he was on the island it was likely that she would run into him from time to time, and it was even more likely that without any help from her he would discover who she was. There was no doubt that as soon as he heard her surname he would connect her with the illustrious painter. And would it matter if he did? He wasn't the sort of man who would come storming up to the villa demanding an interview. Even if he was a writer he wasn't that kind of writer; not a newspaper correspondent, but a literary hack who turned out semi-travel books mixed with a dash of history. Down-grading him in this fashion gave her an obscure sense of comfort. Harney was a literary nobody who mattered to her not at all. Introducing him to the *kolo* dance was the merest act of island hospitality. Without her help he would probably never hear of Urbino, which so far had remained undiscovered by the

41

few foreign visitors. The young Romaines hoped it never would be.

It occurred to Jennie as she swung the car into the villa driveway that Glyn Harney's book on Zelen might in some way be linked with tourism. A possibility which hadn't dawned on her before. She pushed the unwelcome thought away from her. It took time for a book to be written and then published—a year at least. By then all the signs were that tourism on Zelen would be advancing anyway. Already a huge second hotel was being built on a beach the north end of the island. The days of Urbino's isolation were no doubt numbered. Which was a pity—but all the more reason for enjoying it while it lasted.

She found Gervase dawdling over a solitary breakfast on the terrace, where she joined him after putting away the car and delivering her shopping to the kitchen. It wasn't usual for him to be up and about so early and he answered her cheery, "Good morning, Ger," with a sombre grunt.

"I was supposed to be going to the market with you this morning," he reminded her reproachfully. "You promised you would wake me up in time."

"Oh, Gervase, I'm sorry. It completely slipped my mind! I was late starting and had to rush off in a hurry." With a mysterious urgency, she might have added, which effectively banished poor Gervase from her thoughts.

"You forgot all about me," he accused sadly. "Have you also forgotten that this is my last day here?"

She had. Tomorrow Gervase was being taken by a powered fishing trawler to the nearest village on the mainland. From there he would go by road to the airport at Dubrovnik to catch a plane to the French Riviera where he was to join his parents who were cruising the Mediterranean with yachting friends. An arrangement Jennie had greeted with a sense of relief of which she was a little ashamed. Poor Gervase, she had been pretty mean to him throughout his fortnight's stay at the villa, fending off his youthful devotion. She must try to be nice to him during his last few hours on the island.

"Let's go off for a picnic on our own this morning," she suggested. "We could take a boat and row over to Luka." A tiny island about a mile from Zelen. Entirely uninhabited. As children she and Gervase had often played 'Robinson Crusoe' there. It wasn't very beautiful, little more than a rocky atoll, but its miniature sandy beaches provided shells of many kinds and the rock pools abounded in especially beautiful sea anemones and other exotic forms of marine life.

Gervase's face lit up. "That will be super, Jen! And perhaps I could take you out for a farewell dinner tonight. Just the two of us. What about the inn at Urbino?"

Jennie groaned inwardly. Give Gervase an inch and he would take an ell. "You can't possibly go out to dinner on your last night at the villa," she reminded him. "Papa wouldn't like it." Adrian Romaine demanded certain standards of behaviour from his guests, even if they were 'family'. And being present for the evening meal was something he insisted upon, save on rare occasions when an outing had been arranged well in advance to celebrate a birthday or such like. For Gervase to have been absent from the dinner table on his last evening would have been unforgivable.

"Hell!" he muttered rebelliously. "Why does your father have to be so stuffy? Everyone gives in to him."

"I know," Jennie admitted. "But that's how it is. He's old and a bit difficult at times, but we love him and hate to hurt him. Can't you be satisfied with our picnic on Luka this morning?"

Gervase grinned and cheered up. "The picnic will be grand . . . but I'm never satisfied, Jennie, where you are concerned. You know how I feel about you."

"No, I don't," Jennie retorted. "You imagine you've got a bit of a thing about me, but the first exciting girl you meet on the Riviera you'll forget all about me."

"You don't really believe that," Gervase said sadly.

"But I get the message, Jen. I ought to. It's been transmitted often enough."

It wasn't a very promising start perhaps, but nevertheless their day on Luka was an unqualified success. Marie had packed them a generous picnic basket so that there was no need to return home for lunch. The mile-long journey in the rowboat pulling against a strong current was enough to make them pleasantly tired—so that it was bliss just to lie mindlessly on the sand, sunbathing, before plunging into the crystal clear water for a swim. Afterwards they searched for shells and clambered over the rocks, exclaiming at the discoveries they made in one pool after another—a routine familiar through the many summers they had shared on this halcyon coast. They both forgot to be grown-up, dissatisfied, unhappy. There was nothing in the world but the clear golden air and blue green sea.

When they had eaten the good things Marie had provided they rested side by side in a shady cove. Lying face downwards, her head on her arms, Jennie refused to let any disturbing thoughts mar the moment. Her rendezvous with Glyn Harney tonight, John's letter, with its electrifying plans, hidden away in her dressing table drawer—plans that to her drowsy sun-soaked mind still seemed unreal. Soon she must tell Papa . . . Claire . . . all of them, that John wanted them to be married in the autumn. But there were six days to go before he arrived in Zelen, so there was no hurry. She could keep the startling news to herself a little longer.

Rowing back to Zelen harbour in the late afternoon they were both half drunk with sun and sea, drowsily relaxed. Dressing for dinner (another civilised custom Adrian Romaine fostered) Jennie put on a new trouser suit of apricot-coloured silk jersey . . . the exact shade of her suntanned skin and bronze-gold hair. With a tan like that one didn't need make-up, but she took special pains with her eyes, skilfully emphasising the long curling lashes, shading the lids. It made her look older than her twenty years, gave her an air of sophistication which ought to help to keep the Harney man in his place! Not that she was putting on all this eye shadow, and so on, for *his* benefit, she hastily assured herself.

She wondered as she sat at the dinner table if she would be able to slip out of the house after the meal without too many explanations. Not that there was anything to explain. In this Bohemian household folk went their own ways, and few questions were asked. After dinner Adrian disappeared into his studio, taking Jean Duprès with him. Jacques invited Gervase to a game of billiards, and Claire said she was going up to the nursery to have a look at the sleeping Dimples, since it was Nannie's evening off.

"Do you think I might borrow your car?" Jennie asked her, following her into the hall. "It's smaller and easier to handle on the narrow roads than the Cortina."

"Of course you can have my car," Claire agreed, adding with sisterly directness, "Where are you going?"

"To Urbino. I'm taking a visitor I met in the town this morning to see the dancing," Jennie answered in a carefully casual tone. "A writer. He's doing a travel book of some kind on islands and wants to include Zelen in his series. I gather he's here for a week or two—a man called Harney."

"Harney," Claire echoed absently, as they paused outside the nursery door. She was hoping that Dympna, who could be troublesomely wakeful at times, would have safely 'dropped off'. "Harney," she repeated. "The name is vaguely familiar. I feel I've heard of him somewhere. Are his books well known?"

"I'm not sure," Jennie said. "He gives one the impression that he doesn't think they're very important. But that may be his modesty. They're published by the Kingfisher Press."

"Oh, well, it all sounds very learned and respectable," Claire said. "I suppose it's all right for you to go off into the wilds with this unknown male."

"Of course it is," Jennie declared emphatically. "Don't be so early Victorian!

"I haven't said anything to Papa about going out,"

she added then. "You know how suspicious he is of strangers on the island, especially strangers who write."

"He and Jean will be in the studio deep in discussions of designs and techniques until midnight," Claire said. "It's this huge canvas of the cathedral Papa is working on. He can't leave it alone. He's killing himself over it," she added with a worried little sigh.

"He won't miss you. You go off with your Harney man and have a good time."

It was all proving just a little too easy, Jennie felt guiltily, as she turned the car out of the drive and headed for the harbour. It was a gorgeous car to drive, an open sports model, superbly sprung. The soft evening air flowed all about her gently, stirring the strands of bronze-gold hair on her temples. The car was a sort of bronze-gold too. Everything followed the same colour scheme, it occurred to her ... the car, her hair, the apricot trouser suit, her sun-gold skin. Mr Harney should be impressed, she thought wryly. But not too impressed, she hoped. Anyhow, the open car made for less intimacy. What a train of thought! Was she scared of Harney? Yes, she admitted frankly to herself; she was. Or if scared was too strong a word, she was a mite uneasy. Those lyrical things he had said to her when he had run into her this morning. Though 'run into' wasn't quite the way to put it. He had admitted to hanging about the quayside in the hope of finding her doing her shopping.

She would, she resolved, keep their contact this evening on a strictly formal level ... that is if she could manage it. Harney wasn't exactly a manageable individual. Oh, dear, what had she let herself in for in this impulsive rendezvous?

Swerving round the last turn in the descending, winding road, she came out on to the quay. The sun was just on the point of dropping below the watery horizon, flooding the whole scene on land and sea with an unearthly radiance. The evening waterside promenade of the towns-people was in full swing, all the little shops

46

and *kafanas* lit up. In the distance the Slavonia was a blaze of light, the muted throbbing of its dance band just discernible. Nearer at hand someone was strumming a guitar.

Jennie saw Glyn Harney, who had obviously been on the lookout for her, coming towards her. The slanting sunrays shone full on his face. Perhaps it was that which gave him an illuminated air . . . a radiance. He looked so happy, and once more she wasn't sure about his age. Happiness seemed to take years off him.

"So good of you to come," he greeted her formally. "I hardly believed you would."

"But I promised I would," she reminded him, leaning over to open the offside door of the car.

He got in beside her. "What an evening!" he said. "This incredible light. And you look as though you're a part of it . . . a golden girl, not quite real."

She met his too intense glance and laughed aloud. "Oh, I'm real enough, and very matter-of-fact, may I remind you."

He nodded. "I know. No poetic flights of fancy allowed. I'll remember . . . and behave. I'm really very grateful to you for giving up your time to drive me to Urbino."

She did not answer him, preoccupied with turning the car and sending it roaring up the steep incline which would take them to the main road on the east of the island. The sunset light was now behind them, dramatically picking out rocks, trees, wayside flowers. But the whole effect was unexpectedly bleak as they approached the stony spine of the island. Occasional goats and donkeys cropped the sparse grass in the small enclosed fields. Here and there was a lonely cottage, its tiny plot of land planted with grape vines and olives. The general impression was one of poverty and struggle.

"Sad country," Glyn remarked. "It comes as a surprise after the luxuriance of the coast."

"The coast with its belt of woodlands is sheltered from the terrible Adriatic winds which blow here in the winter," Jennie explained.

47

"Do you live here then during the winter?"

"Oh, no," Jennie replied quickly, and then hesitated. Where would a pursuit of this topic lead her? Then, because the play of secrecy and mystery was beginning to feel a little foolish, she said, "We live in London during the winter."

"We?" he questioned.

"Yes," she agreed shortly—and left it at that.

"Just-Jennie, with no surname, no address," he murmured. "Am I not yet to be honoured with a more adequate introduction?" There was a mocking note in his voice.

Jennie's feeling of foolishness increased. Was there really any good reason why she should not tell this man who she was? Even if it meant anything to him that she was the daughter of Adrian Romaine and that the great man was here, painting, on the island, she could not imagine him, on the strength of this discovery, rushing up to the villa to force his acquaintanceship upon her father. He wasn't that sort of person she persuaded herself once more; he was serious, mildly an historian, a writer of educational travel books. And above all he gave the impression of being civilised ... in other words, a gentleman.

She said, "If I'm being a bit obscure about my background, please believe there's nothing personal in it. It's simply that my father, who's not young, spends his summers on Zelen for the sake of its peace and quiet. He doesn't much care about meeting strangers...." She broke off the inadequate explanation, glad to concentrate upon avoiding a flock of geese who at this moment had decided to cross the road. She had to stop the car and wait for them, as with slow and comical dignity they passed on their way, their heads held defiantly high, while their leader, opening a large yellow beak, emitted a series of sardonic squawks.

It was so funny that Jennie and Glyn laughed aloud. With the road clear of geese at last, they moved on and almost at once rounded the bend in the road which led them into the village. "Urbino," Jennie announced, with an air of relief. For the moment the troublesome subject of her identity could be forgotten.

They slowed down before a long, low, whitewashed building with the words 'Khotel-Restoran' painted over the door. A long wooden table flanked by a backless bench stood on each side of the door, close to the house wall. Both tables were partly occupied by the young people of the village.

"We'll leave the car over here," Jennie announced, edging her way to a shady patch under the pepper trees which enclosed a wide square, the inn forming its south side. Beyond the trees the country looked more verdant than the barren slopes they had climbed from Modice. Though it was growing dusk it was possible to make out the neatly terraced land with its vegetable patches, olive groves and rows of grape vines. Obviously, the hills which surrounded Urbino sheltered it from the worst of the winter winds.

Glyn, looking about him with interest, followed Jennie back to the inn. The evening's diversions were already in full swing, the young men and girls at the tables laughing and talking, with pitchers of some kind of drink before them, their glasses well charged. There was a movement among them as the strangers approached, a shifting of places to make room politely for the newcomers. One or two of the girls smiled shyly at Jennie, as though in recognition and there was a general murmur of, "*Dobro vece*!"—Good evening.

A rugged-looking character in shirt sleeves and apron appeared in the doorway.

"*Gospodin, Gospodjica*!" he called in greeting, and then with obvious recognition, and breaking into English, "Ah, Mees Jennie! You are welcome."

"Good evening, Stefano," Jennie returned, holding out a hand which the innkeeper shook enthusiastically, his glance going enquiringly to Glyn Harney.

"I've brought an English gentleman who is visiting Zelen and wants to write about it," Jennie explained. "He was hoping he might see some dancing this evening ... the *kolo*, perhaps."

"A writer!" Stefano, echoed, impressed. He offered his hand. "Glad to know you, sir ... and the dancing we will arrange. Meanwhile. ..." he waved them to a vacant place at the table, "what will you have to drink?"

"Some of your lovely *ruzica*," Jennie said, and turning to Glyn, "That's a sort of delicious light rosé they make here."

"From our own grapes," Stefano added with pride. "Very *lak* ... how you say?"

"Light," Jennie translated.

"Perhaps too light for the *Gospodin*. I would recommend to him the *visnjevica*."

"A liqueur made from black cherries," Jennie supplied.

"A little later," Glyn decided. "The rosé will be fine to begin with." He gave Jennie a quizzical glance. "We mustn't give the infant too much alcholic refreshment, must we? These Slavonic liqueurs are pretty fierce."

"Infant!" Jennie repeated in an offended tone. "What age do you think I am, then?"

Harney laughed. "Young enough to resent being considered young."

"Well, I'm exactly twenty, if it's of any interest to you."

"It is. Everything about you is of interest to me."

She let that pass as they took their places at one of the tables. Stefano had by this time come back with a jug of wine and two tumblers. As soon as he had poured a drink for each of them the young people at the table with them raised their own glasses and there was a murmur of "*Ziveli!*" and "*Sve najbole!*"—roughly meaning, "Cheers!" and "All the best!"

"*Prosit!*" Glyn responded, raising his tumbler. "Won't you have a drink with us?" he invited the landlord, who said he would be honoured, and produced another tumbler.

"Madame Lemaître is not with you this evening," he said to Jennie presently.

"She had to stay with the baby," Jennie explained. "It's the nurse's evening off."

50

"*Ach so,*" Stefano murmured. "And your honoured father? He is well?"

"Very well, thank you," Jennie answered. Any minute now Stefano would be blurting out the family name. But the dangerous moment passed. Some summons from inside the inn made Stefano hurry away.

The light had almost gone from the evening sky by this time the square was full of shadows. The illumination from the windows and doorway of the inn made patterns of brightness on the dusty ground beneath the gently moving tree branches. High over the distant hills the first stars appeared. Someone began to sing—first it was one voice, a girl's, then another voice joined in, a man's, and soon there was a chorus of young voices filling the quiet air with a strange wild music. There was passion in it, and rhythm . . . a dancing song. Stefano was standing in the doorway of the inn again, and when the song ended he said something to the singers in quick unintelligible Serbo-Croat. There was a murmur that sounded like approval and an older man sitting at the far end of one of the tables produced an accordion and played a few tentative chords.

"They're going to dance!" Jennie clasped her hands in anticipation, leaning across Glyn to watch the young people as they moved out on to the square. Though they were mostly in everyday working clothes, having obviously come in from the fields and farms round about, most of the girls wore voluminous aprons and coloured kerchiefs tied round their heads. Stefano had switched on some extra lights and the square was now clearly visible, a pool of golden radiance under the pepper trees. Forming a ring, the dancers began their ritual movements. Hand in hand they circled, going faster and faster to the music of the accordion, the men stamping their feet to emphasise the rhythm. First one way and then another the ring turned, the dancers swinging their bodies. It was exhilarating, exciting. The faces catching the light were vivid, arresting, with their high cheekbones and deeply set eyes, the strongly boned Slavonic feature of the men, the softer, more Italianate delicacy

51

of the women's looks. Through light and shadow they moved, austere and mysterious as the faces on some Byzantine mural.

Though nobody wore national costume on this ordinary workaday summer evening the whole scene had a strange foreign beauty. Glyn Harney watched it, entranced.

"What a picture!" Jennie heard him murmur, as if to himself. "What movement, what design! Imagine this in colour!" And then, turning to her, "Do you think I could ever persuade them to do all this again some time in native dress? When my photographer arrives."

"I'm sure they would be only too delighted," Jennie replied, pleased by his enthusiasm. She was glad the evening was being such a success. It made her feel warm and proud, as if she herself had contrived the whole scene in its village setting for Glyn Harney's especial benefit. Glancing at his lean, absorbed face she was conscious of a deep satisfaction. Just sitting here at his side in the warm summer night, listening to the haunting music of the accordion filled her heart with a peace it had never known before. There were no tensions, no nagging little worries, no past and no future. This perfect moment was enough.

When presently a young girl broke the circle of the dancers to lean towards them, her hand held out, Jennie, responding to the invitation jumped up from the table, her own hand held out to Glyn, drawing him with her into the circle of dancers. After that it was pure magic, the swift exhilarating movements, the impelling music with its exciting rhythms, the same tune repeated over and over again until it achieved a mesmeric effect. So that in the end Jennie was dancing in a trance, her fingers locked in Glyn's, his strength sustaining her, turning her this way and that as the ritual demanded.

It went on until, at last, exhausted the dancers sat down at the trestle table and Stefano brought fresh jugs of the cool delicious wine, small glasses of strong cherry liqueur. But the young people did not rest for long. There was a fiddler now, drawing them to their feet again. This time the dance was not so rapid and they sang as they danced. Heaven only knew where they got the breath . . . and the energy, Glyn remarked to Stefano.

"And this after a hard day in the fields," Stefano pointed out. "We are strong people up here in the hills," he added with pride. "We have to be, we have been forged by a long history of hardship and invasion . . . But nothing has ever conquered us. Not even poverty and the harsh winds of winter."

"What grist to my literary mill !" Glyn said when the innkeeper had returned indoors to his bar. "How can I ever thank you enough for making this unique occasion possible?"

Jennie's spirits soared. "You don't have to thank me. I've enjoyed it every bit as much as you have."

"Nevertheless, I think I ought to be taking you home." He glanced at his wristwatch. "Do you realise it's long past midnight? What will Madame Lemaître be thinking?" There was a quizzical tilt to his dark brows, a hint of curiosity in his tone. "Your mother?" he hazarded.

"My married sister," Jennie said.

"So you're not a Lemaître?" There was no attempt to mask the curiosity now, and Jennie, unable any longer to keep up her reticence, answered, "My name is Romaine."

"Ah !" The long drawn out monosyllable held significance.

"Does it convey anything to you?" she could not resist asking.

His glance held hers for a moment. Was it triumph or some strange gleam of amusement in his unwavering look? "I'll say it does ! There can be only one Romaine who hides himself away on an Adriatic island to escape publicity."

"Then you knew he was here?"

"I had a pretty good idea he might be."

"But you didn't realise I was his daughter."

Later, much later, it was to occur to her that Glyn

53

Harney's reply to this was equivocal ... not quite straight. "I might, if I'd connected you with Romaine, have taken you for the great man's granddaughter," was what he said.

"My father, as I expect you know," Jennie told him, "has been married twice. I belong to the second marriage."

"Then the writer, Karla Burnett, is your mother?"

"You know her?" Jennie asked sharply. How familiar was this stranger with her family's history? Was it possible that he was, after all, in some way connected with the dreaded world of gossip writers and news gatherers?

"I know *of* her, of course," Glyn Harney was replying. "Her novels are extraordinarily fine."

But a casual reader of them would not necessarily connect the pen name, Burnett, with the painter Adrian Romaine. At the same time, Jennie argued with herself, if Glyn Harney was a fan of her mother's, an ardent admirer of her writing, it would be natural enough for him to have learned something of her personal life. He didn't have to be a newshawk because he knew she was married to the famous painter.

"She's in the States at the moment, lecturing," she said, offering this information as a bait. If Glyn Harney rose to it and revealed that he already knew of the American lecture tour her suspicions of him would be reinforced. But all he said was, "So that's how you come to be keeping house ... doing the family marketing?"

"Something of the kind," Jennie agreed shortly, and standing up said they had better be on their way. "But first I must say goodbye to Stefano," a courtesy which took up several minutes during which Glyn Harney asked the innkeeper what chance there might be of seeing the *kolo* danced in national costume.

"Any Sunday evening, or holiday," Stefano told him. "The old customs do not die on Zelen. Nor need we wait for a holiday. If Miss Jennie would let us know when you are likely to be coming to Urbino again. ..."

"The old boy obviously has a soft spot for you," Glyn

remarked when they were in the car. "Do you come to Urbino very often?"

"Quite often," Jennie confirmed.

"An admirable subject for your father's painting, I should have thought . . . the dancing, I mean. . . ."

"It's not quite his thing," Jennie murmured. "Not abstract enough, though no doubt he could convey something of its meaning in the abstract." An involved reply. Was it silly of her to be so suspicious of Glyn Harney, imagining that every question he asked had some sinister journalistic implication?

"But obviously he paints here on Zelen?"

"Of course. Painting is his whole life . . . that and entertaining his friends. Many of them come to stay with us."

"The famous and successful," Glyn hinted with what seemed to Jennie a touch of wistfulness, so that she answered, "My father isn't interested in fame and success. Many of his friends are poor and struggling painters and writers, from Chelsea or the Left Bank in Paris. He doesn't judge or classify people. He just likes them as they are." She threw Glyn Harney a wary glance and could not resist adding, "The only type he can't abide is the publicity-seeker, or paid exploiter—sharp-nosed gossip writers and journalists with their shoddy values. These he abominates and avoids like the plague."

"Hence the summer hideout on Zelen," Glyn Harney said. "It's understandable. To be pursued eternally by the vulgar for reasons which are wholly vulgar and superficial must be intolerable."

"It is," Jennie agreed. "And the latest horror is publishers bothering him to write his memoirs. Something he simply refuses to do, since he hates writing. He says his paintings must be his record."

Glyn Harney said earnestly, "I'm sure he's right." And then, even more earnestly, "Do you suppose I might ever be permitted to see the work he's engaged upon here? Perhaps he would take pity on me as one of the struggling writers . . . and also one of his lifelong admirers."

55

Jennie's heart gave a lurch. How quickly he had seized on this opportunity to work his way into the Romaine circle! Or was she just being needlessly nervous? It was quite natural for Glyn Harney to want to see something of Adrian Romaine's work, not from idle curiosity, or as a news-gatherer, but because he, Glyn Harney, was himself a man who appreciated beauty, who had spoken as a painter or a poet might have spoken when she had been with him in the little cathedral.

"As long as you didn't put him in your travel book," she said hesitantly. "He would hate to be listed as one of the 'sights' of Zelen for sensation-hungry tourists."

"Good lord!" Glyn exclaimed, "I wouldn't dream of such a thing. What do you take me for? One of the news vultures?"

"I . . . just wondered," Jennie faltered.

"Well, stop wondering and give me the benefit of the doubt. I'm simply a poor hack, earning an honest living, recording backgrounds. Making rather long captions for photographs, if you like." Another cue missed, she was to reflect later.

They were high on the hillside now, the road descending steeply before them. Stars were beginning to pale in the light of a waning moon just appearing over the shoulder of a mountain on the distant mainland, its rays bringing to the warm, scented night the final touch of magic. Far below lay the lights of Modice and, as they watched, the moonbeams touched the waters of the bay with silver.

Jennie felt Glyn Harney's hand cover her own as it lay on the wheel. "Let's stop here a moment," he suggested. "It's so beautiful."

When she switched off the engine the sudden silence brought a sense of utter peace. Leaning back in her seat, Jennie gazed up into the infinite sky, darkly blue, throbbing with stars. "You can almost hear them singing," she whispered. "Is it true that the stars in their courses sing?"

"The music of the spheres," he said. "Pitched in a key too high for our mortal hearing."

Bringing her gaze back to earth, Jennie was suddenly, vividly aware of the man at her side. Still lying back on her seat, she turned to look at him. In the mysterious half light his face was grave and still, his eyes, meeting her glance, were filled with a strange sadness. In the long look they exchanged she felt her very bones dissolve, her heart lying still as a snared bird in her breast. Then with gentle deliberation he leaned over her and kissed her. The singing stars whirled about her. There were no thoughts any more, just the drowning, mindless ecstasy. It was not a very prolonged kiss, nor a very passionate one. But life would never be quite the same again. No other kiss had ever been like this. As he drew away from her she looked up at him in bewilderment, as if she were waking from a deep dream. And she didn't want to wake. Life would come rushing back at her with its dread implications. If only she need never *think* again!

"You wanted me to kiss you, didn't you?" he asked softly.

"Yes." The single word came out half a sob, half a sigh.

He laughed. But it was an indulgent little laugh .. kindly, understanding. He put a hand on her arm. "Dear Jennie, you're too beautiful . . . too young!" The sadness was in his voice now as well as in his eyes. "I must take you home. You're tired. I'm the one who ought to be doing the driving. Do you think I might—would it help?"

She pulled herself together at that and answered a little sharply that she was quite all right and perfectly well able to drive. "I can drop you off at the *kafana*," she told him briskly.

"But that's taking you out of your way," he pointed out. "Put me down when we reach your hilltop home—which must be close by now—and I'll make my own way down the hill to the harbour."

They argued about it for a little while and in the end

he persuaded her. At the gateway to the villa he got out of the car and she showed him the path through the trees which was a short cut to the harbour.

"When may I see you again?" he asked as he took his leave.

"I don't know! I don't know!" she cried wildly, and starting the car with a jerk shot through the gateway and up the villa drive, leaving him standing there looking after her.

CHAPTER FOUR

TAKING the car round to the garage in the courtyard, Jennie was so flustered in her thoughts that she didn't at first notice that all the lights in the house seemed to be on. What on earth was going on? And why at this time of night should the kitchen door be flung wide open? Vaguely alarmed, she hurried indoors. Marie was leaning over the stove stirring some liquid in a saucepan. She was wearing a dressing gown and her grey hair hung in wisps about her drawn and haggard face.

Barely glancing up at Jennie, she said drily, "A fine time for you to be gadding off, staying out half the night!"

"Is something wrong?" Jennie interrupted uneasily.

"I'll say something is wrong! Your father had a serious heart attack round about ten o'clock and the whole place has been in a ferment ever since . . . Monsieur Lemaître racing all over the island in search of Dr Sinjek. He wasn't available at his home . . . dining out with friends, and the friends, if you can believe such a thing in this day and age, had no phone."

"But Father?" Jennie burst out in an agony of apprehension. "How is he now? Has the doctor been?"

Marie, as if glorifying in the drama, and determined to prolong the suspense, shook her head. "I can't tell you how your poor father is. I only know that the doctor has been and gone and I'm now making a little bouillon for Madame Claire to give the invalid during what's left of the night." She glanced significantly at the old-fashioned clock on the wall, which with a laborious wheeze struck 'two'.

"Is it really as late as that?" Jennie murmured guiltily, and without waiting for an answer: "Do you think I might go up and see Papa?"

Marie shook her head portentously. "You'll have to

ask Madame Claire. But I can tell you one thing... they would have been very glad of the Ferrari you went off with when they were tracking down Sinjek. It's so much faster on the road than the Cortina."

Not waiting for any more direct or implied reproaches, Jennie shot out of the kitchen and long the passageway which led to the front hall. Claire was coming down the stairs with an enamel jug in her hand.

"Oh, Claire!" Jennie moaned. "Marie has told me... it's so awful I wasn't here. How is Papa now?"

"Over the worst of it, we think," Claire returned. Her tone was blessedly brisk and optimistic after Marie's lugubrious utterances.

"I wouldn't have gone out if I'd known...."

"Of course you wouldn't, lovey. Don't look so tragic. There wouldn't have been much you could do if you had been here."

"What did Dr Sinjek say about him? Can I see him?"

"You can peep in for a moment or two, I expect. He isn't asleep. I'm just going to get some boiled water to dilute a sleeping medicine Sinjek left for him—it's just a sort of tisane, I think, some sort of local peasant remedy Sinjek has faith in. He says Father should be all right if he rests for a week or so and there are no further attacks. He has ordered oxygen for him. Jacques has gone to the hospital with Sinjek to collect a cylinder."

"Oxygen!" Jennie said in a frightened voice.

"It's to help his breathing. Don't look so scared. Sinjek doesn't seem to be seriously alarmed—so we must try not to worry. Luckily we shall have John here in a few days and he'll tell us what we ought to do and whether it's necessary for Papa to be moved back to London for more expert care."

John!

The name struck Jennie like a blow over the heart. She went up the stairs with leaden feet, her sense of guilt so overpowering that it was suffocating her. John and her father—tonight she had failed them both.

The sickroom was one of the larger bedrooms in the villa, ornately furnished with a huge, draped four-poster bed. Already it smelled of hospitals, Jennie thought. Only one low-voltage lamp burned on the bedside table. Adrian Romaine, propped up on pillows, lay with his eyes closed, breathing a little unevenly! His face in the shadows was waxen, his eyes sunken and dark-ringed. Perhaps he was asleep after all. Jennie was preparing to creep out as quietly as she had come in when the sunken eyes opened.

"Ah, Jennie-wren, you've come home at last. I'm glad you missed all the fuss this evening. Quite unnecessary fuss, most of it. Have you had a pleasant time?"

If the tone was husky and rather weak the words were reassuringly normal.

"I had a lovely time, Papa," she answered absently.

"Come and tell me about it." He held out his hand. Warm with relief at finding him apparently so nearly his usual self, Jennie tiptoed forward and sat herself gingerly on the edge of the big bed.

"You don't have to creep about like a scared little mouse," her father laughed. "I'm not all that ill. Have they been scaring you with stories of my collapse? All that happened was that I passed out in the studio in the middle of a session with Jean. We were discussing the validity of symbolism in painting, and suddenly I blacked out. I expect I've been overdoing it a bit lately, working too many hours on that huge canvas of the cathedral. And I've been swimming more than is wise, old Sinjek says. He's ordered me complete rest for at least a fortnight; but I can't think of anything more boring. We'll see if your John has any more acceptable advice to offer when he arrives on Tuesday."

Jennie nodded. "It's marvellous that he's coming. He'll know what you ought to do," she said a little breathlessly.

"He'll want me to get back to London to see his revered father, perhaps. But I can't see myself going all the way to London in the middle of our lovely summer here—just to have Davenham give me the once-over. I'm not dying yet!"

In spite of the brave defiant words the voice was beginning to be a little more weak and husky.

"You're talking too much," Jennie warned.

"I expect I am," he agreed unrepentantly. "But it's so boring lying here, feeling wide awake. Claire is making me a medicinal tisane, which Sinjek says should make me sleep. Meanwhile you can tell me what you've been up to. Claire says you've discovered a lone historian wandering about the island, studying the local lore for some book he is writing. You took him to Urbino."

"Yes, I did," Jennie agreed. "I wanted to show him the girls and boys dancing the *kolo*."

"Where did you meet this character ... how did you come across him?"

"Down on the quays when I was doing the marketing the other morning," Jennie returned vaguely, still repressing the story of Glyn Harney's intervention when she had been hurt by the careless crane-driver. She could hardly tell it now, having kept quiet about it yesterday.

"Then this morning I ran into him outside the cathedral," she continued. "I went in with him while he looked round. He talked knowledgeably about the architecture and seemed to know quite a bit about Yugo-Slav history."

"You mean he connected the history with the cathedral?" Adrian asked.

"Yes, I think so. He spoke of the various foreign invasions of the island and the mark they left on island life. But what I noticed most was his feeling for the beauty of the cathedral. He said at one point, 'Only love could have built this place'." Her voice was soft as she repeated the words. She heard her father murmur an appreciative "Ah!" on a long breath. And then, "What about his writing? Did he tell you anything about that?"

Jennie nodded. "He's doing a series of what sound like more or less popular books on the islands of Europe. He's done Sardinia and Corsica and the Greek islands. Now he's doing the Adriatic islands."

"All of them," Adrian marvelled.

"Probably not. Just the more important ones. We didn't go into details. He may simply be doing Zelen."

"He seems to be approaching it in the right spirit. I like what he said about our little cathedral: 'Only love could have built this place.'" The old man repeated the words musingly, his gaze losing itself in the shadows beyond the small circle of light from his bedside lamp. "I wonder if he would care to see my painting of the cathedral?"

Jennie drew in a sharp breath. Her father's unexpected suggestion had thrown her into that ridiculous state of confusion which everything connected with Glyn Harney seemed to generate. She had been startled enough when he had asked if she thought he might some time be permitted to see her father's paintings, and she had nervously fobbed him off, leaving the matter vague. It had seemed to her unlikely that her father would welcome the stranger's intrusion... and here he was inviting it! Why did the thought frighten her? The last thing she wanted, she discovered then, was for Glyn Harney to come to the villa. A reaction she did not stop to examine. But instinctively she felt that Harney was entering into her life and environment with altogether too much ease. She didn't want it that way. The less she saw of Glyn Harney, the better. In a confused way she was aware of this as she countered her father's impulsive, "Ask him to lunch, poppet."

"But you're supposed to be resting, Papa. Don't you think you ought to wait until you're a little stronger before you see strangers?"

Adrian Romaine made an impatient gesture. He wasn't accustomed to having his ideas questioned; he liked getting his own way. Here in his own home his word was law.

"All this fuss about a slight heart attack!" he begun indignantly. "I'm not suggesting that I get up and entertain this friend of yours. You and Claire can give him lunch and then he can come up here and have a chat with me. In a few days, when I'm about again, I could show him my mammoth canvas of the cathedral. Meanwhile I think you ought to get off to bed. It's very late and you're looking extraordinarily peaky all of a sudden. What did you say this man's name is?" he asked as she stood up.

"Harney," she answered in a small voice. "Glyn Harney."

Adrian shook his head. "Never heard of him. But ask him to lunch nevertheless. Tomorrow . . . or as it's already tomorrow probably the next day would be best."

Claire came in with the jug of steaming tisane. "Here's your hot drink, Papa . . . and Jacques has just come back with the oxygen cylinder, which will make it easier for you to breathe."

"It's not all that difficult now," Adrian remarked crossly, man-like hating all this sickroom fuss. But as he sat up to accept the cup of tisane Claire had poured for him it became evident that he was much weaker than he cared to admit. Supporting him with an arm, Claire held the cup to his lips.

Feeling more alarmed at this little tableau than at anything which had happened since she had heard of her father's attack, Jennie murmured a subdued, "Goodnight then, Papa darling!" and crept from the room.

The sight of Jacques coming up the stairs with the bulky oxygen cylinder robbed her of the last shreds of her composure.

"Oh, Jacques, how bad is he really?" she asked brokenly.

"Bad enough," Jacques returned, resting with his burden at the top of the stairs to answer her. "But Sinjek assures us that with rest and treatment things should right themselves. The heart, Sinjek says, has wonderful recuperative powers."

But Jennie wasn't really comforted. "I wish I hadn't gone out tonight," she sighed.

"You couldn't have done very much if you had been at home," Jacques said, just as Claire had done. It was true, of course, but small consolation. She watched her brother-in-law pick up the oxygen cylinder and make his way down the corridor to the invalid's room, then she turned into her own bedroom, shutting herself in with her uneasy thoughts.

She was quick as she could be getting into bed. Just for a moment it was bliss to lie there in the dark—the world shut out. She was achingly weary. If only she could go straight to sleep, her mind blessedly blank! But the mixed emotions of the long day came crowding in on her. It was the shock she had received when she came back to the villa tonight that was uppermost. The frightening news of her father's sudden illness, and the agony of guilt it brought her—an illogical guilt, she told herself. The fact that she had gone to Urbino with Harney had nothing to do with her father's heart attack. Indeed, she persuaded herself, it had nothing to do with anything. It had been no more than a kindly impulse— taking the stranger to see the dancing. Her father had appeared to accept it as perfectly natural—little more than a gesture of polite hospitality to an island visitor. Why then should she be in such a tizz about it?

That kiss on the hilltop in the moonlight—she forced herself to think about it calmly. Such a casual little kiss—no more than a salute to the moment's romantic beauty. Why must she give it any importance? It couldn't be compared with the hot young kisses she and John had exchanged on occasion. John! Why, oh, why should the thought of him make her heart ache so intolerably? The tears were suddenly hot behind her closed lids. It had been such a mixed-up sort of day . . . drifting about the lovely little cathedral in the early morning with Glyn Harney, hearing him say he had been hanging around the quayside hoping for a glimpse of her. The drowsy hours with Gervase—poor Gervase lying on the sand at her side—the long sun-gold day but a prelude to the evening when she would go with Glyn Harney to Urbino.

Had it really been like that? If so it was because Gervase could be so boring—and Glyn Harney wasn't boring; a bit of an enigma. Sensitive to the island's beauty, sophisticated, far too much of an intellectual to be writing popular little snippets of history for the hoi-polloi. What was his real purpose in coming to Zelen? It was her curiosity he excited, she told herself firmly, and felt the tears wet on her cheeks. Wiping them away, she settled herself resolutely to sleep. In a little while it would begin to get light. She *must* sleep now if she was not to be a total wreck in the morning. And she mustn't be a wreck. There was her father to care for, her father needing her.... She clung to that, telling herself that her father was the most important person in her whole world ... more important at this juncture even than John. Consoled indefinably by the thought, she slept.

It was disgracefully late when she awoke the next morning—almost ten o'clock. Peering at her bedside clock, she rubbed her eyes unbelievingly. But it had been all hours when she went to bed, she excused herself. The events of the previous day came rushing at her. Papa! How was he this morning? Jumping out of bed, she hurried over her morning toilet and went along the corridor to be met by Claire coming out of the invalid's room.

"Papa?" Jennie began breathlessly. "How is he this morning?"

"He had quite a good night," Claire told her. "I sat up with him." She stifled a yawn.

"Oh, Claire, why couldn't I have done the sitting up?" Jennie asked hungrily. "At least you could have let me help you. We could have taken it in turns."

"There wasn't that much left of the night," Claire reminded her sister. "And anyway, I'm off to bed now. I'll go up to the spare attic where I won't be disturbed by household noises. Nannie has taken Dimples down to the beach to keep her happy and out of the way."

"I'll see nobody makes any noise," Jennie promised. "Is Papa asleep, or should I go and sit with him?"

"The nurse who has just arrived is with him," Claire said.

"A nurse?" Jennie echoed in alarm.

"Dr Sinjek thought he'd better have one. There are

injections to be given, and so on, and she should be able to keep him quieter than we could. She's from a nursing order of nuns, and seems sweet, but could be quite firm, I imagine, which is what Papa needs." With another yawn Claire went on her way to her attic hideout.

Jennie ran down the stairs and out on to the terrace to find Gervase sitting disconsolately at a littered breakfast table.

"I thought you were never going to get up," he reproached her. "In a very few hours I've got to catch that wretched boat. Do you think I ought to go, now that Adrian has been taken ill?" he added hopefully.

"Of course you must go," Jennie declared, with unnecessary vigour. "What good could you do if you stayed? You would only be another burden for Marie, who's already a bit flustered by Papa's illness."

"A burden," Gervase said bitterly. "Thanks very much."

Jennie poured herself a cup of half cold coffee. "I wonder if anyone did the marketing yet?" she mused.

"I did," Gervase put in virtuously. "At least, I took one of the maids down in the car and waited for her while she shopped around. Marie, in fact, asked me to do it. She knew it was no use waiting for you to wake up after last night's excitement."

"Excitement, is hardly the word," Jennie reproached him. "Everyone was terribly worried. You didn't hear a thing, I suppose, up there in your room in the roof."

"I went to bed about ten and slept like a log until seven this morning," Gervase admitted. "Somebody might have called me and told me what was going on. But you were out for most of the time, it seems." He eyed her narrowly.

"Yes, I was," she agreed briefly, and hoped they might leave it at that. But Gervase was not to be so easily put off.

"I don't know how you can be so mean, Jennie," he sighed. "Refusing to spend the evening going out to dinner with me and then haring off with some stranger. Claire told me about him—some old boy who's delving into the troubled history of Zelen for a book he's writing."

"I didn't go out until after dinner," Jennie reminded him, "and then it was simply to give Mr Harney a lift to Urbino where he wanted to see the dancing."

Some old boy delving into Zelen's troubled history! she thought with wry amusement. Was that really what Claire imagined Glyn Harney to be? Or was it Gervase's idea?

"Oh well," he was saying bitterly, "I expect you enjoyed it more than you would have enjoyed being stuck here with me. I expect it's just as well I'm pushing off today. I don't suppose anyone will miss me. I'd better go upstairs and pack."

Jennie, ignoring the self-pity, said, "Try to be quiet moving about your room. Claire has gone up to the attics to get some sleep. No transistor music this morning, for instance."

"Do you take me for a complete fool?" Gervase flung at her in justifiable outrage. "With Adrian ill and Claire who's been up all night trying to rest. . . . Honestly, Jennie!" Words failed him.

"I'm sorry, Gervase," she offered contritely. "If I'm being tactless and stupid this morning it's because I'm worried about Papa."

Seizing on her softer mood eagerly, Gervase said he was practically packed anyway and what about a quick dash to the beach for a last swim?

Still feeling remorseful at her treatment of Gervase, ashamed because she was so relieved he was going away, Jennie said she would love to swim with him, and a few minutes later they were on their way to the beach.

It was just after lunch when she took him in the Cortina down to the quay to catch the boat. It was blazingly hot at that hour and apart from the small stir around the departing trawler the place was deserted; Zelen deep in its afternoon siesta. Would Glyn Harney too be resting? Somehow she couldn't imagine him sleeping during the day. He would scorn such a weakness.

Glancing over at the *kafana*, Jennie wondered if when Gervase had gone she might call and give Glyn his invitation to lunch. Would he realise how honoured he was? She herself still couldn't quite believe it was happening. She had told Claire about it and Claire had asked the doctor when he called that morning if a visitor would be harmful for the invalid. Dr Sinjek had said, no, as long as he didn't stay too long. Monsieur Romaine seemed to be making excellent progress, he had pronounced, and was already well on the way to full recovery. It was this and this only that was making her walk on air, Jennie told herself. Glyn Harney's invitation to lunch had nothing to do with it.

"You might at least try to look a little sorry I'm leaving," Gervase said, as he kissed her goodbye.

"I'm sorry, Ger," Jennie fibbed. "But there's no need to go all melancholy about it. You'll probably be back again in almost a month."

"Sure I'll be back," Gervase emphasised, "and one of these days I'll make you take me seriously."

She wasn't even listening, having just at that moment caught sight of Glyn Harney about to descend the long flight of steps from the higher level of the town. By the time Gervase was on board and the little boat was on its way Glyn had reached the bottom of the steps and was making for the *kafana*. Hadn't he seen her? Jennie began to hurry towards him. But he walked resolutely on. To run, to call out to him would have been just a little too eager. But surely he was aware of her—hadn't she detected one of his quick glances when she reached the level of the quay and turned towards the *kafana*? His not stopping to speak had puzzled her, but there was no time to work it all out. She was almost level with him now and he had reached the *kafana* door. Half turning his head, he raised his hand in a hurried little salute, then walked into the *kafana*, shutting the door behind him—all but slamming it in her face. Jennie stood thunderstruck, her heart plummeting. If ever there had been a snub direct! But why? Why? she asked herself, horrified at the sharpness of the pain which swept through her. As though a snub from Glyn Harney was the end of the world!

Slowly she walked back to where the Cortina was parked. Turning inland she drove up the hill, her mind seething with questions. Why the sudden change in Glyn Harney's attitude? Yesterday morning he had, on his own admission, wandered about the market place hoping to find her. And this afternoon he had quite plainly turned his back on her. Was it because of that kiss last night? The quick shamed colour flooded her cheeks. "You wanted me to kiss you, didn't you?" he had asked with a cool detachment she had been too overcome to notice at the time. Now, recalling the words, she read the scorn into them. He thought she was cheap... pursuing him, offering her lips to a man she scarcely knew. There had been nothing in their evening together to lead up to that kiss. They had watched the dancing, even taken part in it—but it was more a romp than an amorous exercise. They had drunk a little of the pungent red wine—at least she had drunk only a little, and Glyn, she noticed, had been equally abstemious. So it could not be said they were unduly intoxicated, excited. Then on the way home they had stopped the car to listen to the silence and watch the moonrise. He had kissed her... and with all her heart she had responded to his touch. She had not sought the depth of feeling which swept over her, and tried to dismiss it now as a sudden infatuation. She wasn't in love with Glyn Harney. How could she be? A man she had only just met and who could mean nothing to her. Love was the feeling she had for John—a warm, quiet happiness based on long association and dear familiarity. That was the good love, the lasting love. The facile emotion Glyn Harney aroused was a midsummer madness. She must put it away from her. And the fact that Glyn himself seemed disinclined to continue their tenuous acquaintanceship would make it all the easier. In a few days John would be here and everything would be normal again. John, the man she was going to marry before the leaves of summer had fallen from the trees.

John! She repeated his name again and again, like an invocation, a prayer to banish all evil spells and wild enchantments.

As she approached the house she overtook Nannie and Dimples just emerging from the short cut path through the wood. They were returning from their second long session on the beach and the child was tired. "Mama ... I want Mama!" she cried fretfully as Jennie stopped the car to pick them up. Poor spoiled little Dimples, who always got her own way, but today she had been banished from her mother's side for hours at a time, her usual routine interrupted.

Jennie, absently summing up the small domestic upset, found it difficult to think of suitable things to say, either to the young nannie or her little charge. It was as though she had been away from them for aeons of time ... away in another world, so that everything pertaining to her everyday life had become unfamiliar.

Claire met them on the terrace, warning them to be as quiet as possible. Adrian, after his brief night and a restless morning, was having a prolonged afternoon sleep, induced by a tranquillising injection. "You'd better give Dimples her tea in the summerhouse at the end of the garden," Claire told Nannie—an arrangement that displeased Dimples. Feeling she was not the centre of her mother's solicitude, she emitted a series of the high-pitched squeals which never failed to get her immediate attention.

Claire succumbed at once, fearful that the shrill sound would disturb the invalid. "All right, darling," she soothed. "Mummy will come and have tea with you in the summerhouse."

"Oh, Claire," Jennie couldn't help expostulating, "you spoil her so, giving in to her fits of bad temper."

"It isn't bad temper," Claire explained in a long-suffering tone of voice. "I've tried to make you understand this before. It's simply the poor little scrap's very wholesome way of asserting herself—establishing her identity in the big vast world. Anyway," she added hurriedly, "I can't let her scream the place down with

71

Papa sleeping. I was going to have tea with Sister Therese. Will you take her on instead? Marie is sending a tray into the salon. Sister doesn't like eating out of doors, it seems."

For the next half hour Jennie was kept busy entertaining the quiet little nursing sister. Later she spent some time at her father's bedside. He looked better and seemed refreshed after his long sleep.

"Did you find your historian today?" he asked. "Is he coming to lunch tomorrow?"

She had hoped he would forget the stranger, but no such luck. This odd insistence upon Glyn Harney's being invited to lunch! It was all part of the queer sense of fate which seemed to be dogging her.

"No, as it happens I didn't get a chance to speak to him," she answered evasively. "I was busy with Gervase all the morning, and then helping Claire this afternoon. No doubt I'll run into Mr Harney again before so long," she ended in an offhand way.

A reply which appeared to satisfy her father. Probably he would forget all about Glyn Harney now, Jennie thought with a stab of pain. Because it didn't look as if she was ever going to get the opportunity to convey that luncheon invitation. And it was better that it should be so.

Conversation wasn't exactly animated over the dinner table that evening. It was a weary household, all of them feeling the reaction after the shock and upset of Adrian's seizure the night before. By ten o'clock there was a general movement towards bed. Jennie went up to say goodnight to her father, but was met outside the door of his room by Sister Therese who said she had already settled him for the night and he ought not to be disturbed.

Jennie obediently turned away, but found herself reluctant to go to her own room so early. The prospect of being shut in alone with her thoughts dismayed her. All the afternoon and evening she had pushed the image of Glyn Harney away from her, refusing to let herself remember her sharp dismay when he had cut her dead on the quayside. Going downstairs, she drifted out on to the terrace. It was the magic hour when twilight dies and the last of the summer brightness has gone from the June sky. The air was cool with the falling dew, flowers and grass and trees drinking in the blessed moisture after the burning heat of the day. She would walk through the little wood to the top of the cliff path and take a last look out over the sea, she decided. It would steady her nerves, bring her perhaps to her senses. She drew in great breaths of the pure, refreshing air, a faint breeze beginning to stir, coming straight from the sea. Perceptibly her nerves relaxed. Why had she made such a thing about Glyn Harney's cavalier treatment of her this afternoon—reading all sorts of complicated meanings into it? Perhaps he had had some reason for hurrying into the café. . . important writing to get on with, an expected phone call. Why did she imagine that she was in any way important to him? Quietly she reasoned with herself.

She had come to the end of the little wood now, the cliff path before her. There was no surprise in her heart when she saw Glyn standing before her, tall and silent and very still as if he were waiting for her.

"I knew you would come," he said. "I willed you to come."

He held out his arms and she went into them.

CHAPTER FIVE

FOR a timeless moment they stood clasped together, their heartbeats mingling, not tempestuously, but gently, as if everything in the world had suddenly come right and never again would there be any cause for fear or doubt. At least that was how it seemed to Jennie. She wondered if it was the same for her companion and heard him say, "Oh, Jennie, this is all wrong! This isn't at all the way I meant to greet you this evening." But he did not let her go.

"I saw the look on your face when I turned away from you this afternoon," he said. "It was as if I'd struck you! I couldn't forget it."

"Is that why you came looking for me tonight . . . because you pitied me?"

"No," he answered. "Because I feared for you . . . and for myself." He loosened his hold on her, standing a little way from her. With a finger tip under her chin he raised her face, small and pale in the deepening twilight.

"Last night when I kissed you something happened between us . . . something more perhaps than either of us intended. It's better that we should be honest about it now; to ourselves and to each other."

Jennie's eyes widened and darkened. What was he telling her? That last night's kiss had mattered to him too? She could hardly breathe for a moment; the implication was so startling, so unexpected. This wasn't the easy technique of 'chatting up' but something far more, and he had spoken of honesty.

"Let's walk along the path a little way," he said. "I've got to talk to you, Jennie darling. You're so sweet, so young. . . ."

As if that were a disadvantage!

"You aren't exactly a Methuselah yourself," she laughed, and suddenly she was filled with an almost unbearable happiness. Glyn had sought her out tonight, climbing the dark hill. "I willed you to come to me," he had said.

"I'm thirty-four," he was answering her Methuselah quip.

"And I'm twenty."

They were moving along a level stretch of the path, the rough land on either side thick with rosemary and thyme. Sea and sky melted together, violet-coloured in the gathering darkness. The first stars were small and white and very far away.

"It isn't only a question of ages," Glyn said. "You know nothing about my background."

"Is that important?"

"In this case, I think, yes. Vitally important." He hesitated an instant, and later she was to remember that significant pause. If he had been completely frank with her then it might have saved her some of the pain which was to come.

But all he said when he continued was: "I'm not the sort of person with whom you ought to become seriously involved. I'm not flattering myself you're *likely* to be seriously involved. But there it is; a word of warning. We mustn't get things out of proportion, my dear. You spoke of the island's magic the other day, and told me I must not get my personal feelings mixed up with it— very sound advice. If I shut the *kafana* door in your face this afternoon perhaps it was because I was trying to act on it. Then I saw how much I'd hurt you. It shocked me ... scared me a little." He paused and then said softly, sadly, "You mustn't fall in love with me, Jennie. It would never do."

Her fragile happiness was shattered, yet mixed with the pain was the wonder that they should be talking to one another in this way. Discussing a love they must not encourage (for hadn't he implied it could be mutual?). That such a love could exist, even as a remote possibility, was so wonderful that she could hardly take it in.

"We've only just met," she began. "And yet ... and yet ... when you kissed me last night. . . ."

"Don't go on!" he put in sharply. "There are things we must not say to one another. Things left unsaid make the situation so much easier . . . and safer. I'm nothing to you, a passing stranger. I have my life, and you have yours. You are committed to other friendships than mine, I have no doubt. That good-looking boy you were seeing off on the trawler this afternoon?"

"Gervase," she supplied. "My sister's husband's young brother. Gervase could never be important to me . . . in the way you mean."

"But there is someone who could?" he probed.

John! She knew then that in all loyalty she must speak of him. To deny him by silence would be a betrayal of the meanest sort. And Glyn had asked for honesty.

"There's my fiancé," she said, in a tone from which all life had gone. "He's arriving on the island on Tuesday."

"Well, that's fine!" Glyn declared bracingly, with what could so easily have been a vast air of relief. If there was a mild emotional problem between them John had solved it.

They had come to the end of the path and turned round. "So this is where we go our separate ways . . . freed from our island magic," Glyn said. "I'll leave you at your gate, Jennie dear, and if I keep out of your way in the future you'll understand. No morning coffee in the market place, no more drives to Urbino. Which doesn't mean I'm not grateful to you for the kindness you've shown me. But now it had better be goodbye." They had reached the villa gateway. He held out his hand.

"But it can't be goodbye," Jennie heard herself blurt impulsively, adding almost without her own volition, "My father wants to meet you." It would have been so much wiser to have left the words unspoken.

"Your father?" Glyn sounded thunderstruck.

"I told him you were here to write a history of Zelen, and of your interest in the cathedral. Which happens to be his most absorbing interest too just now. He's paint-

76

ing an immense abstract of it, and thought he would like to show it to you. He would like you to come to lunch tomorrow."

She heard him draw in a sharp breath. "But this is stupendous! How can I thank you?" In his enthusiasm she felt he had moved far away from her. And he had completely forgotten his decision that they should not meet again.

"You don't have to thank me," she said quietly. "You'll be doing my father a kindness if you come to see him. He's ill at the moment, and forced to rest in bed for a few days. This he finds boring. He's not a good invalid. It would be a help if he had someone like yourself to talk to."

"But this is too wonderful! I'm knocked sideways ... overcome with the honour of it all. ..."

"Then we may expect you tomorrow; about noon?"

"I'll say you may!" He put a hand on her arm. "And it's all your doing, clever Jennie! This is far more than I ever could have expected or hoped for when I set out for Zelen." Another remark she was to remember later. Just now she could only feel that she had suddenly become of secondary importance to him. She was no longer the Jennie with whom he must not become emotionally involved, the Jennie who touched his heart. She was Jennie the daughter of the celebrated painter, the elusive Adrian Romaine—now, by a miracle, not so elusive. And that, Jennie felt, was all that mattered to the man now peering absently at her in the pale starlight. Even the touch of his hand on her arm conveyed a chilling impersonality. And as though the chill were palpable as a cold wind, she shivered.

"It was to give my father's invitation that I chased after you to the *kafana* this afternoon," she said. If it wasn't the whole truth it helped her hurt pride. "If you'd known I was bringing you this invitation," she couldn't resist adding, "you wouldn't have shut the door in my face, would you?"

A question he left unanswered, and he didn't even have the grace to look embarrassed by it.

Later, as she tossed and turned in her bed trying to assess the earlier part of their conversation on the cliff top, the answers she came up with brought her little comfort. Glyn Harney, mildly attracted to her, she concluded, had been alarmed by her too enthusiastic response. So he was warning her off, saying there were factors in his background she would not like. What factors? Why be so mysterious about it? If he were married or engaged or in any way committed, why not say so right out? But he had preferred to be vague, fobbing her off. All those veiled hints about his background. Trying to get rid of her, she supposed, without hurting her pride too much. "You mustn't fall in love with me, Jennie," he had said. Had she indeed showed her feelings last night so plainly? And was she falling in love with him? Of course not.

But it was a long time before she was able to sleep, fighting the mixture of emotions which threatened to overwhelm her. It was her affection for John which was the reality in her life, she reminded herself again and again. Glyn Harney could mean nothing to her. If he had briefly attracted her it was no more than an accidental physical attraction she must ignore. Something born of the magic of a midsummer night ... and like a midsummer night it would fade in the everyday light of her ordinary existence.

Adrian Romaine was so much better the next day that the doctor permitted him to leave his bed for a few hours and lie in a comfortable lounge chair by his open french window. As he was just above the terrace he was able to observe the comings and goings of the family. Dympna's noisiness did not worry him, he declared; indeed he liked to hear her vigorously asserting herself, queening it over her compliant elders. He wasn't an 'easy' patient, Sister Therese had pronounced. It was difficult to get him to remain in the placid state of non-being which she regarded as the complete rest the doctor had ordered.

When Jennie looked into his room during the morning he persuaded her to stay with him for over an hour reading a four-day-old copy of *The Times*.

Was she going swimming with Claire and Jacques this morning? he asked when at last she laid the newspaper down.

Long ago they had set off without her, Jennie forbore to point out and said instead that she had thought it best to stay around so that she would be on hand to receive Mr Harney when he arrived.

"Ah, yes, your wandering historian," her father said. She had already told him that Glyn had accepted the invitation to lunch. "He seemed very excited at the prospect of seeing your paintings," she said now. "But perhaps you wouldn't want him to see them until you yourself are able to get to the studio to show them to him."

"Oh, no," Adrian disclaimed. "I'd like him to have a look at my cathedral painting before you bring him up here. Then I can talk to him about it." It was one of the largest canvases he had ever attempted, an ambitious and extraordinarily complex composition.

"That exquisite little building," he mused aloud. "If it's the history of Zelen he wants he'll find so much of it there. The church that is the heart of the island, guarding in its stones the faith and hope of almost five hundred centuries."

"You really must rest now, Signore Romaine," Sister Therese declared, coming into the room with a cup of the inevitable bouillon.

"When am I to be allowed something more interesting than this eternal carrot water?" Adrian grumbled.

"There is a milk pudding to follow," Sister Therese told him encouragingly. "And you must not despise your bouillon," she added sternly. "It is far from being carrot water, being made from Marie's excellent chicken stock." Plain, middle-aged, dedicated, the face under the flowing nun's coif held a reassuring tranquillity. Though he grumbled at her, Adrian was glad enough to accept her, depending upon her skill and knowledge and gentle discipline to see him through this strange valley of shadows into which he had stumbled. Only he himself knew how near he had been two nights ago to passing right through that valley to the mystery which lay on the other side. Pain and darkness had engulfed him right there in his familiar studio in the midst of a conversation with his old friend Jean.

Now, humbly accepting the hated broth, he waved his goodbye to Jennie as she turned at the doorway to blow him a goodbye kiss. "I'll come back after lunch with Mr Harney," she promised.

"Not until the *signore* has had his afternoon rest," Sister Therese insisted. And then his visitor must not be allowed to remain too long.

Out in the corridor Jennie stood still, halted by the wave of anticipation which swept over her. Glyn Harney. Ever since she awoke this morning she had been waiting for the moment when he would arrive. Going to her room now, she lingered a while, gazing absently at her reflection in the dressing table mirror, making small ritual movements, brushing her hair back from her brow, touching her lips with an almost colourless salve. But she wasn't thinking of how she looked, every nerve in her body waiting for the sound of a footstep on the path beneath her window. How would she face Glyn Harney? How would they greet one another this morning? Was it only last night he had held her in his arms, only to tell her she must not love him?

Glancing through the open window, she saw that he was coming through the gateway at the end of the drive. Her feet seemed to scarcely touch the stairs as she hurried down to the hall, and then out on to the terrace where he stood tall, and unsmiling in the shadow of the trellised vines which tempered the heat of the midday sun. They looked at one another in silence. Ordinary words of welcome seemed inadequate.

"So you've come," Jennie managed at last.

Glyn Harney smiled. "Yes, here I am!" They did not move towards one another, did not shake hands. A strange inability to hold normal conversation seemed to possess them.

"My sister and her husband haven't yet come back

from their morning trip to the beach," Jennie offered.

"And your father? I trust he's feeling better today?"

"Much better. He's sitting up by his window. He's looking forward to seeing you after lunch, after you've paid a visit to his studio and had a look at his painting of the cathedral."

"Ah, yes, the cathedral," said Jean Duprès as he joined them. "An extraordinary *tour de force*. . . ."

Jennie introduced him. Glyn Harney shook his hand warmly. "I admire your work, Monsieur Duprès," he announced—rather to Jennie's surprise. Jean Duprès' sculpture was abstruse, eccentric, designed to appeal only to those initiates who appreciated the extreme in experimental art. And he was little known outside France. Harney must be well informed if he had even heard of Jean Duprès. He was not only an historian, it seemed, but a connoisseur of contemporary sculpture at its most daringly modern.

"I'll fetch some drinks. Won't you sit down?" she invited, and left them talking together ensconced in two of the comfortable wickerwork loungers. In the salon she assembled bottles and glasses on the cocktail trolley, inwardly blessing Jean for his timely appearance. And what a mercy Glyn Harney knew of his work—a factor which should take care of what might have been the awkward period before lunch.

As she wheeled the trolley out on the terrace she saw with relief that Claire and Jacques were coming up the path from the cliff top, damp of hair and glowing with sea and sun. There were more introductions. Drinks were poured, and conversation blossomed afresh.

And presently Jean was announcing that he would be leaving them on the following day when the steamer called. "You must not burden yourself with guests when you have illness in the house," he answered Claire's protests.

"But my father will miss having you to talk to him about his painting," she urged.

"Monsieur Harney will no doubt be occasionally visiting him," Jean pointed out. "And from what I can

81

gather he will be at least as knowledgeable an art critic as I am."

They ate in the cool, shaded dining room. The meal, simple, but perfectly prepared, was served by Yanna, one of the local girls who helped Marie in the kitchen. Sister Therese in her white coif sat at the table with them, but took little part in the flow of talk. Neither did Jennie, listening to Jacques holding forth on his pet topic—the value of the cinema as an art form. Once more Glyn appeared to be interested, and extremely knowledgeable about film production and direction. Either he was really an expert in this field, or an extraordinarily adroit conversationalist.

A man of the world, brilliantly clever and sophisticated. How could she ever hope to hold his attention ... or any deeper emotion? Now the things they had said to one another last night in the starlight seemed wildly impossible. So did the swift flare-up of feeling which had given rise to the things they had said. The whole happening seemed now to Jennie totally unreal. This time last week she had never heard of Glyn Harney!

And yet ... and yet! As she watched him talk with Jacques, a dapple of light and shadow from the latticed blinds crossing his strong but sensitive face, her heart knew indefinable pain.

"Shall we have our coffee on the terrace?" Claire suggested.

It was another half hour before the little group broke up and Jennie was free to take Glyn to the studio. And once more when they found themselves alone an awkward silence fell on them.

"The studio is quite a long way from the house," was all Jennie had to offer as they crossed the garden. Flowers and trees drowsed in the afternoon heat. Glyn yawned—audibly—and hurriedly apologised, "That deceptively mild Dalmatian wine we had at lunch must be stronger than one suspects!" he laughed.

But Jennie wondered bleakly if it might be boredom with his companion, as well as the deceptive wine, which had made him yawn. There was no doubt that he was set on keeping her at a distance today...if indeed he thought about it at all. He had been lively enough at the table, talking with Jean and Jacques, now and then bringing Claire into the conversation, with the deference a polite guest shows towards a hostess. But not one word and scarcely a glance had found its way in Jennie's direction.

If we could just have been friends, she thought sadly. If I hadn't spoiled everything by being too forthcoming. Filled with shame, she remembered how easily she had gone into his arms last night when he had said, "I willed you to come to me," a remark she had probably totally misunderstood. It might simply have meant he had been anxious to see her so that he could explain why he had shut the door of the *kafana* in her face, an impetuous gesture he had regretted.

Fumbling a little with the large key, she unlocked the door of the studio and led the way into the darkened interior, lit by a series of skylights over which thick green blinds had been drawn. It took Jennie a little while to pull the long cords which folded them back, Glyn offering to help her. The small shared task seemed to ease the tension between them, and Glyn was instantly alert, looking about him with interest. Built of local stone and immensely solid, the studio had at one time been some kind of barn or outhouse. Years ago when he first came to the island Adrian Romaine had converted it into an ideal studio, and now it was filled with the clutter inseparable from an artist's work. There were canvases stacked by the dozen, face against the wall, a long pinewood working bench, paint-stained and littered with palettes, and palette knives, tubes of paint and jars of brushes. The air was redolent of paint and turpentine.

But as the light poured in with the blinds drawn back one object dominated all else; a vast canvas covering one entire wall.

"Good heavens!" Glyn exclaimed, as he gazed in amazement at it, his dark head thrown back. Two high step-ladders supporting a scaffolding of planks revealed the way in which much of the work on this mammoth canvas had been carried out.

"The effort that has been put into it!" Glyn marvelled. "No wonder your father has knocked himself out. It would be an herculean task for a man half his age."

In silence then he studied the details of the painting. The colours were superb, reproducing the soft glow of the cathedral marble, the harmony of design in the flying buttresses. And woven into the whole was a patchwork of patterns in which the faces and forms of people and animals appeared. There were pastoral scenes, battle scenes, history and allegory, fact and myth mixed together—but all without confusion. A world contained in the fabric of a single building, and beyond the building with its golden spires, a landscape breathing peace and tranquillity, where no battles were fought, no warriors fell from stampeding horses. Here there were olive groves and cornfields, and between walls of crumbling marble, by a broken font, children played.

It was some time before he turned from his scrutiny of the picture with a long sigh. "It's like some great closely packed book," he said. "I would have to live with it before I could begin to take in all that it has to say."

"I know," Jennie agreed with sympathy. "Though I've looked at it many times I'm still lost when I stand before it."

But Glyn did not answer her, still gazing at the painting. She did not exist for him at this moment, and he had quite forgotten the yawn-making effect of the Dalmatian wine. The painting like a great bugle call had roused him to life, filled him with the excitement which only a work of genius can evoke. And Jennie was glad that it was so, though she couldn't imagine the great picture having any lesser effect on him. Where matters of art were concerned he was vulnerable, easily reached and influenced. This was one of the things about him which had attracted her so strongly.

She said, "My father wouldn't expect you to take it all in at a glance. But you'll have seen enough of it to enable you to listen with understanding to what he has

84

to say about it. It's his latest work and means a great deal to him."

He turned a dazed glance at her. "I'm honoured that he should want to talk to me about it. I can hardly believe in my good fortune."

There were many other canvases, but he did not want to look at them. "Not just now," he said. "I don't think I could take in any more for the moment. The impact of that giant canvas is . . . terrific!"

"And my father will be waiting for us," Jennie reminded him. When he helped her to pull the blinds back in place, his hand was over hers. Light was blocked out. In the shadowy studio with its great brooding canvas they stood still, facing one another. A current of feeling passed between them. Hold me, Glyn! she longed to cry out. Hold me close to you. Let me feel your heart beating with mine, your kiss on my lips.

He saw the quiver that passed across her face, and it was almost as if she had spoken the wild words aloud. The glance they exchanged was deep and defenceless, utterly without self-consciousness. Raising a hand he let it move gently, as a blind man might have done, tracing the outline of her brow and jaw. Then with a finger tip he touched her eyelids, first one and then the other, closing them. "It's easier when I can't see your eyes," he said, and turning, he walked before her out into the glare of the afternoon sun.

He's *not* indifferent to me, she thought, following him. Even if his interest in me is little more than a passing fancy some feeling about me does exist. But what right, she asked herself bitterly, had she to speculate about his feeling for her one way or the other? She was John's girl. Lost, disloyal, but still John's girl, and somehow she must get her bearings again before the steamer came in on Tuesday morning.

Dimples and Nannie were coming out of the house towards them, the little girl fresh from her afternoon nap. She ran to them, her plump little arms held out. "Man!" she cried delightedly, flinging herself at Glyn, her arms clasped about his knees.

They laughed as he bent to caress the child's bright curls.

"Do all women fling themselves at you like this?" Jennie asked, still laughing. Just as I did, she might have added.

Perhaps he added it for her. His glance was quizzical as he picked the little girl up. "Only the very young and beautiful," he answered.

Dimples, her arm about his neck, gazed at him adoringly. "Man," she murmured to herself in a satisfied tone. "Nice man!"

"Much as I appreciate the compliment," he said, putting her down gently, "I'm afraid we have to be on our way. Your grandpa is waiting for us."

"Grampy," she echoed. "Poor Grampy sick."

"Exactly," Glyn agreed. "That's why we mustn't keep him waiting."

With an understanding nod Dimples submitted to being led away by her nannie.

"You handled that little crisis perfectly," Jennie couldn't help saying as they went into the house. "Dimples was all set to ride about indefinitely on your shoulder. And she can raise merry hell if she doesn't get her own way. But the way you explained your action to her was just right."

He offered no comment on her word of praise, merely saying, "She's a lovely kid. Your niece, I suppose."

"Yes," Jennie said, with the odd little sensation which invariably came to her when she realised she was an aunt! A maiden aunt at that.

Adrian, in his lounge chair on the balcony beyond the french window, greeted them enthusiastically. Above his violet and gold dressing gown—an Emperor's robe—his face was grey and drawn, only the eyes full of life; the keen all-seeing eyes of a painter, summing up the younger man as Jennie introduced him.

"You're working on a history of our island, I hear," he opened the conversation when Jennie and the visitor were seated on the chairs Sister Therese had left ready for them. Waylaying them in the corridor outside the sickroom, she had warned them that they must not tire the patient by staying too long. "His spirit is so much greater than his strength," she said.

He seemed all spirit now, talking of his beloved island. He had spent every summer here since soon after the war, he told Glyn. "I knew it before the war, way back in the thirties. It was something of an adventure to come here then, for it was all fairly primitive and in many respects very poor. One could still see the results of years of imperialist domination." He spoke of the proud and patient peasant people tilling the land for the crops on which they subsisted. Harsh laws from their overlords crippled fishing, which was a major industry.

"It was not unusual to meet beggars, who incidentally begged with great dignity, not only in the town, but far out in the country where we went for long walks—my first wife and I. They were not really roads under our feet but cattle tracks, and there were no cars. Now, with their own very individualistic form of Socialism, things are much better, more prosperous. With their Slavonic courage the people of Zelen, like the people on the mainland, have triumphed over years of foreign conquest and kept themselves inviolate."

It was after a pause that he added thoughtfully, "I've tried to put something of all this into my painting of the cathedral. Has Jennie shown it to you?"

"She has indeed!" Glyn confirmed, and haltingly he tried to express something of what he had felt when he looked at the great work. He spoke of the eloquent faces in the painting, the battle scenes, and the ultimate triumph of the peaceful background landscape.

"They have never been conquered, these people," Adrian said. Then dropping his voice dramatically, "Until now. For the first time they're in real danger, not from war, but from peace. Go and look at my painting again. In one corner, seemingly insignificant as the lurking bacteria in a body fated to die, you'll see an aeroplane." Once more he paused to shake his head.

"Plans for the construction of an airstrip on Zelen, I'm told, have already been passed. It's only a question of time—a very short time—before tourism will do what centuries of invasion have not achieved, that is the despoiling of the countryside—a gradual alteration of the whole atmosphere of the place. There will be hotels and more hotels, noise, an influx of money, a loss of innocence." He passed a hand across his brow. "I shall not see many more summers on Zelen, if any."

"You mean because of modernisation," Jennie put in sharply. The hint of despair in his tone frightened her. Was he more ill than she knew? "There are lots of other quiet places where we can spend our summers if you tire of Zelen," she declared brightly. "And anyway, it's going to take some time before that air strip is made."

"Not so long," Adrian said. "Already the great new hotel being built on the other side of the island is almost ready for its occupants. Oh, the visitors will soon be upon us ... in their hundreds. And it's right that it should be so. People who work hard in sad northern climates have a right to their share of sunshine and to the exotic resorts which for too long have been exclusively enjoyed by the rich and privileged. But it's sad to see the old ways go."

"I've come, it would seem," Glyn said, "just in time to capture some of the spirit of the old Zelen before it vanishes."

"This will give your book an added value," Adrian suggested. "I'm glad you are writing it ... this summer which perhaps is Zelen's swan song. And mine," he added under his breath. "There are times in this strange and changeful age when I'm glad I'm at the end of my life, not at the beginning."

"Oh, Papa, really!" Jennie expostulated. "There's no need to talk like this, just because you don't feel very well and a new hotel is being built on the island."

Good temperedly, Adrian laughed at himself. "Perhaps I am being a trifle morbid," he admitted, giving Jennie a reassuring smile. "But I don't like women in long white veils who keep me shut up in my room, and order me about. And speak of the devil...."

The bedroom door opened and Sister Therese

appeared, long white veil and all. "You have talked with your visitors long enough, Signor Romaine," she announced firmly. Then turning to Jennie and Glyn, she added, "I must ask you to go now."

"What did I tell you!" Adrian groaned, making a comically rueful grimace. "I'm being bullied to death in my own house...killed by kindness. You'll come again," he insisted, with a farewell handshake for Glyn. "I've enjoyed our chat. And do let us assist you in any way we can with your island researches. Go and look at my cathedral painting again—and again, if it's any help to you. And I'm sure Jennie would drive you to any place of interest which might be useful to you."

"Of course I will," Jennie agreed, hoping she didn't sound too eager.

"That's very kind of you, Miss Romaine," Glyn murmured formally.

CHAPTER SIX

GLYN HARNEY was not slow to take advantage of Adrian Romaine's cordial invitation. And Claire backed it up, suggesting that Mr Harney might, on occasion, like to go swimming with them at their special secret beach the far side of the island. She had taken to him at first sight, just as her small daughter had done. "He's *simpatico*," she had said to Jennie, the first day he came to the villa. "I hope we shall see a lot more of him while he's on Zelen. It's good for Jacques to have a man of his own kind to talk to."

So it was that during the three days which remained before the arrival of the steamer bringing John, the stranger spent a good many hours with the Romaine family. In the forenoon he would go to the beach with them, and after lunch spend some time on the upper balcony with Adrian. Jennie did not intrude on these sessions, but her father speaking to her about them later, disclosed an increasing liking for the young man.

"He has the true historic sense," he said. "With me he agrees that there's no use trying to stem the tide of so-called progress which is bound sooner than later to affect life on our idyllic island. But he's not without hope that the disruption may have something of value to offer. New life comes out of chaos." The old man's voice grew dreamy. "Out of death comes resurrection, out of winter, spring. The phoenix rises from the ashes : the painful and irreversible processes of evolution. And these processes Harney recognises."

"I'm sure he does," Jennie offered inadequately, wondering not for the first time at her father's affection for this man and for the strange fate which seemed to be bringing him more and more into their family life—a fate she could not resist. And if his daily visits brought her a mixture of happiness and misery, nobody guessed.

"I'm glad to talk with him," the old man went on. "He brings me fresh ideas, opens new vistas. Perhaps I have in my latter years become too much of a recluse. But Harney is oddly persuasive. We even talked about my memoirs the other day."

"Your memoirs?" Jennie echoed, with a stab of apprehension.

"Not memoirs in the accepted sense," Romaine explained. "I shall never get down to the laborious tome that's expected of every man who has achieved the smallest degree of notoriety in this restless age, a sort of vulture-cult I deplore—a peering and prying into the writer's secret soul after he has died. The message I shall leave must be found in my paintings. For those who have the eyes to see my whole humble journey through life has been depicted with my brush. I've told Harney this and I feel he understands as few people could."

Was it really so, or was Glyn being extremely astute? Jennie wondered. But there was little opportunity for her to talk privately with him nowadays. She seldom found herself alone with him, and then only for a few minutes. The morning sessions on the beach were happy family affairs, sun-tanned bodies sprawling on the golden sand of the tree-sheltered cove which was their sanctuary. At intervals they would run, calling to one another, into the clear water, to swim and dive. Jacques usually brought underwater equipment of a simple kind, but without breathing apparatus it was not possible to remain beneath the surface of the water for very long. There was just time to dive through the shallows to a sea-bed where there were glimpses of colourful fish, and waving multicoloured weeds.

Jennie, watching Glyn's stripped, muscular body cutting through the blue water, felt an odd desolation, the strange loneliness which so often assailed her these waiting days. It would be a good thing when John arrived. At least the pattern of life would be altered, just in what way she would not let herself explore. The less introspection there was just now, she had discovered, the better.

It was Sunday. On Tuesday that fateful steamer was

due. And Jennie hadn't yet confided in her father or Claire John's wish for an autumn wedding. It was because of her father's illness, she excused herself. The prospect of an imminent marriage would be bound to introduce a certain amount of fuss into the Romaine ménage. And even pleasurable excitement was bad for Adrian just now.

She was lying on the beach soaking in the sun's warmth after a strenuous swim when these thoughts drifted through her mind. She did not welcome them. If only everything in her life was as sleepy and peaceful as it seemed outwardly at this moment. But so soon John would be here. She tried to imagine their meeting on the quayside with the early morning stir of the market all about them. Vividly she could see the stalls and the bustling women, the white steamer edging towards its berth, but try as she would John remained a shadow . . . a ghost. She couldn't even remember exactly what he looked like. His face was a blur. While with every nerve in her body she was aware of Glyn Harney stretched out on the sand not an arm's length away from her. She only had to reach out a hand to touch him. If they were alone the temptation might have been irresistible.

Burying her face in her arm, shutting out the sunlight, she tried to account for this madness which had overtaken her. For it must be madness! This emotional involvement with a man who was to all intents and purposes a complete stranger. After all, what did they know of him beyond what he himself chose to tell them? And yet here he was haunting her heart, spoiling these lovely summer days for her.

She must keep her mind resolutely on John and what they would say to one another when he arrived. Obviously one of the first things to be discussed was his plan for an autumn wedding. If her father was on the mend, as he seemed to be, there was nothing to stand in its way. The thought sobered her, brought her down to earth with a bang. Marriage was basic . . . marriage was real; far removed from the wild ideas which had been pestering her of late. And it was marriage to John she was facing. Dear John whom she had loved for so long.

Perhaps when she saw him on Tuesday everything would come right. The strange spell which had fallen upon her would be lifted. She drew in a long quivering breath which might have been a wordless prayer, and heard Claire's voice calling to her that it was time to wake up and go home to lunch.

Yes, indeed, she thought wryly, it was time she woke up from her crazy dreams!

"You'll come with us, won't you, Glyn?" Claire invited. But Glyn refused the invitation.

"I'm always accepting your hospitality," he told Claire. "Now it's time I offered you some in return. Will you dine with me tonight at the Slavonia ... all of you?"

"But three of us," Claire protested. "And the Slavonia is terribly expensive when you aren't one of their package people."

"I shouldn't let that worry you," Glyn smiled.

There was a little more argument, but finally it was settled. Claire and Jennie and Jacques would drive down to the Slavonia at eight, where Glyn would be waiting for them.

"A nice change from my humble *kafana*," he said.

He hadn't mentioned her specially when he was giving his invitation, Jennie thought, as they drove back to Modice. But sitting beside her now in the back of the car—which Jacques was driving—she turned to find him giving her one of his intent and disturbing looks. "I'm told the dance band is good at the Slavonia," he said. "Do you enjoy dancing?"

She was painfully aware of the swift colour in her cheeks. "Oh, yes," she said, "I love it."

"That's grand," he settled in his seat with a satisfied air. "So do I!"

Taking it for granted that they would dance together—as of course they would. Why make such a thing about it? But the rest of the day was a vague stretch of time to be lived through until the moment of

93

their arrival at the big gay hotel. They would have drinks on the wide smoothly paved terrace with its rows of fairy lights, and beyond it the garden where the original island trees and flowers grew undisturbed, date palms and cacti and aloes with leaves like swords, hiding bright scarlet blossoms. A broad path led to a white beach, bordering the mystery of the night-dark sea. Jennie knew it all by heart. There had been several family celebrations at the hotel since it came into existence two years ago. A birthday party of Adrian's last summer, when he had just managed to escape from the camera of a prowling photographer ... an enterprising young man from the local press.

And John had brought her here more than once.

She switched her thoughts sharply at this point, wondering what dress she would wear tonight. Her gentian blue, she decided, the most sophisticated dress she possessed, with a short deeply cut bodice and a long gracefully full flowing skirt. It would be fun to dress up for once. *Kafanas* and country inns were all very well in their way, but there was much to be said too for luxury hotels with all their modern glitter. And the Slavonia, though there was nothing specially original about its design, was beautifully situated on a wooded peninsula with the Adriatic on one side of it and the harbour of Modice on the other.

Glyn was waiting for them in the flower-filled foyer, a tall sauve figure in conventional white dinner jacket and black tie. There was a quiet assurance about his greeting. Obviously he was a man accustomed to entertaining. With the minimum of fuss he was ushering them across the mock marble floor, through a white and gold dining room to the softly lit terrace, where, as Jennie had foreseen, drinks were served. Her choice was fruit juice. Even aperitifs in Yugo-Slavia can be pretty potent ... not to be recommended if you wanted to enjoy the excellent light wines later on.

It was early in the season and the hotel was not yet as full as it would be in July and August. But it was animated enough with its cosmopolitan clientele. It seemed as if every European language was being spoken around them, including some cheerfully obvious English dialects, north-country predominating.

"And the food is equally international," Glyn warned them. "I'm told you can sample a variety of world-famous dishes here, from English roast beef to Hungarian goulash. But Nikole, my host at the *kafana*, tells me we mustn't miss the lobster."

"A Zelen speciality," Jacques confirmed.

They sat over their drinks while the twilight faded. Dancing in the adjoining ballroom was already in full swing. And later when they went into the dining room they danced between courses, Glyn starting it by asking Claire to be his partner, leaving Jacques to dance with Jennie, a duty dance he performed a little absently, his eye on his wife and her tall distinguished-looking escort. To Jennie he seemed to eclipse every other male in the room, with his dark good looks, his quiet dignity, his air of sophistication.

"Must be costing him a pretty penny this evening," Jacques mused. "Slavonic prices for the non-pension visitor are fairly steep. He must be a successful writer, doing unusually well out of those books of his. I shouldn't have thought potted histories of Mediterranean islands would have been all that profitable." Jacques' tone held a note of doubt. "I wonder what his line of country really is?" A question that was to be answered before the evening was over. But first there was the half dreaded, half longed-for moment when Jennie found herself being guided on to the dance floor by their host.

The band was playing the Englebert Humperdinck signature tune, "Please Release Me ... Let Me Go!" to slow waltz time—a sad little ditty, almost too apposite in the circumstances. Perhaps Glyn found it so, for after they had circled the floor a couple of times Jennie felt herself being gently piloted towards the open doors which led to the terrace.

"Shall we walk across the garden to the beach?" Glyn suggested. "Just for a brief breather. Dancing is a bit strenuous on a hot night like this. . . ." He tugged a little too dramatically at his collar. He need not have laboured the point, she thought. The message was clear enough. In spite of his earlier enthusiasm for the dance band he didn't want to dance with her. The thought hurt.

But when they stood by the water's edge it was if they had come to a different world, where feverish emotions subsided and there was nothing but the quiet sound of the gentle waves which broke at their feet. Behind them were the bastion-like cliffs which supported the old town, the floodlit spires of the cathedral pointing to the distant stars.

For a while neither of them spoke, as though reluctant to break the spell of sea and sky. This was better than the noisy ballroom, Jennie thought, better than dancing. In this starlit quietness there was a sense of intimacy and peace, a feeling that it was right for them to be here together. She slid her hand into his and his fingers closed over it, firm and strong.

"It's so lovely out here," she said softly.

"The right setting for you," he answered. And as if his thoughts had met her own—"Better than that rather garish ballroom. I shall always think of you in Urbino, the village in the hills where we danced with the villagers under the trees to the wild music of violins."

It was as though she was already no more than a memory to him . . . someone to be consigned to the past.

She turned her fingers within his palm. "Oh, Glyn!" she whispered in desperate indefinable appeal.

He put an arm lightly about her shoulder.

"Dear Jennie, this is just a summer night dream—a very sweet one perhaps, but no more than a dream. You know that, don't you? And dreams are made to fade."

"Is it your dream too?" she asked. But he did not answer her, and a moment later was saying firmly that it was time they went back to the others.

Claire and Jacques they found had moved to the terrace for coffee and liqueurs.

"Where have you two been?" Claire demanded a trifle sharply.

96

"Getting a breath of sea air," Glyn returned evenly. "Clearing our lungs of ballroom fug." He turned to the hovering waiter and for the next couple of minutes discussed with Jacques the relative merits of cherry and plum brandy. Jennie, refusing either, ordered plain grape juice.

They chatted in a desultory fashion for a while, Jennie being careful to take her part in the conversation with a forced brightness. At all costs everything must seem normal. It would be dreadful if Claire were to be suspicious of her feeling for Glyn Harney, and in her big sisterly way began probing, asking awkward questions.

Presently one of the dining room waiters came and handed Glyn the bill, tactfully concealed on a silver platter. Glyn leaned over and signed it and with a nod and a word of thanks, dismissed the waiter.

"You have an account here?" Claire exclaimed.

"I have," he admitted in a tone which had become oddly strained and unwilling. "As a matter of fact this evening, before you arrived, I booked a couple of rooms for my two photographers. They'll be arriving on Tuesday's steamer."

"Photographers?" Jacques echoed.

Glyn cleared his throat, took a swallow of plum brandy and looked despairingly around the little group. "There's something I have to make clear to you folk," he began. "As a matter of fact I haven't been wholly frank with you as to the nature of my work on Zelen."

Jennie gave him a swift, startled glance, and in his answering look there was pleading, as if he was begging her to understand.

"You've been writing a series of books or booklets on the history of various Mediterranean islands," Jacques prompted. And then with a laugh, "What sinister purpose lies behind this harmless activity?"

"Quite a lot lies behind it," Glyn said, and straightening his shoulders went on with a resolute, take-it-or-leave-it air. "They're not so much books as ... scripts, for a series of television documentaries I'm to give on a London network at some unspecified date."

There was an electrical silence. A dozen questions seethed in Jennie's mind, but she could not utter any of them. Her tongue felt thick and dry in her mouth.

It was Jacques who spoke first, asking in a cutting tone, "Did you choose Zelen as your Adriatic island because the inaccessible Adrian Romaine is known to spend his summers incommunicado here?"

"I knew of Mr Romaine's summer hideout, of course," Glyn admitted, "and of the number of journalists and publishers' agents and such like who in years past have unsuccessfully pursued him here. It was no part of my plan to follow in their somewhat obtuse footsteps." And after a pause "Believe me, I had no intention of intruding on Mr Romaine's privacy."

"Then you met Jennie," Claire prompted.

Glyn nodded. "Fate and a swinging crane took a hand in bringing us together. From then on the situation developed with an impetus of its own. Astoundingly, I was invited to the villa to meet your father. I was given the freedom of his studio, shown his great painting of the island cathedral, and, please believe me, I would at this point have revealed my true identity only that Jennie had told me how ill her father was and if he had heard of the presence of a television reporter on the island it might have upset him."

"It certainly would," Claire agreed drily. "And *will* when he gets to know about it."

Glyn tugged at his shirt collar, as if he was once more feeling the lack of air he had experienced on the dance floor. "We shall have to be guided by circumstances," he suggested, and looked at Claire appealingly. "It may not be necessary for us ever to tell him who I am. For indeed you may rely on me. Now that I've accepted his extraordinary hospitality and . . . friendship, if that's not too strong a word . . . I feel myself honour bound to consider his feelings in every way."

Claire said, "If you really want to help him the best thing you can do is cancel your Zelen project and find yourself some other Adriatic island for your series. In which case your stay here would seem to him no more than a brief holiday, with a spot of historical research thrown in."

Glyn gave her a hunted look. "But I'm afraid I can't possibly cancel my Zelen project. My contrast specifically includes it in my island series. In fact it's the high spot of the whole undertaking."

"Because Adrian Romaine lives here," Claire put in sharply.

"Perhaps," Glyn conceded. "Though the possibility of interviewing him remained extremely remote and at no time was it my intention to harry him."

Claire maintained a sceptical silence.

"And now, as I told you, my photographers will be arriving on Tuesday and then we shall really get down to work."

Jennie who had been listening to the exchange wide-eyed and shocked, felt as if the final blow had been delivered. John and the television photographers arriving on the same steamer! Somehow that seemed to her the most alarming aspect of the whole deplorable affair. How could Glyn Harney have been so dishonest with her, concealing from her his real purpose in coming to the island? She tried to remember just how he had reacted that evening at Urbino when she told him she was a Romaine. But there was nothing clear in her memory. Cleverly in everything he had said that evening he had fogged the issue. He had not been straight with her. Was this why he had warned her off, repudiating the sympathy which had sprung up between them?

As if echoing her sister's thoughts Claire was asking, "Why did you not tell my sister you were a television reporter that first day you met her?"

"It seemed better not to," he answered evasively. "And she hadn't given me any indication of her connection with the great Adrian Romaine."

Claire shook her head doubtfully. "I still can't understand why you had to be so secretive."

"The arrival of a television team on the island might create some excitement. I dare say it will when my photographers arrive. I didn't want to precipitate matters. Being able to wander around the place incognito, as it were, was more helpful to my research."

"But you could have revealed your television connection to Jennie when you did discover she was a Romaine," Claire emphasised. "I still can't understand why you didn't . . . and I wish you hadn't invited us to dine with you tonight, nor entertained us so lavishly."

"No doubt out of a generous expense account," Jacques put in with a grin.

"It puts us in a very awkward position," Claire went on. "I don't know what my father will say if he discovers you're here to give his beloved island the full publicity treatment. We must try to keep it from him. As you yourself admit, there will inevitably be a good deal of excitement among the inhabitants when you start filming. It might be as well in the circumstances, Mr Harney, if you didn't come to the villa any more."

"Isn't that a bit steep?" Jacques put in, with an apologetic glance towards their host. "After all, this thing seems to have built up without Harney meaning it to. He has given us his word that he will not include your father in his film of the island. And wouldn't Adrian be rather surprised, not to say distressed, if he suddenly vanished without any word of explanation?" He turned to Glyn. "The old boy seems to have taken an extraordinary liking to you. He was telling me only this morning that your insight into his painting of the cathedral has given him great encouragement."

"He's expecting me tomorrow," Glyn disclosed. "To continue our discussion on the cathedral. I've left some notes for him of my impressions of Zelen and how it seems to be linked on so many ways with the beautiful little cathedral which stands at its heart."

"You've been very clever," Clare said acidly, "knowing just the line to take with the old man. I can only hope nothing will emerge from your visits to upset him. Though he's recovering from his recent heart attack we're told by his doctor that we must not take his progress too much for granted. It's of the utmost importance that he should not have any emotional disturbances. Somehow it must be kept from him that you're connected with the world of publicity he abominates. The whole thing is most unfortunate, and once more I must say I think you've been less than honest with us." She stood up from the table. "And now, if you'll excuse us, I think we'd better leave."

It was comparatively early; they had only just finished dining. Claire's withdrawal was so clearly a snub that Jennie found herself going hot with embarrassment.

"I'm sorry our evening must end like this," Glyn said. "But I quite understand how you feel. I hope you'll realise that the last thing I wanted was to put you in an awkward position when I invited you to be my guests this evening. It was a straightforward impulse of friendliness, and nothing more. Then as we talked at dinner I felt that the time had come to tell you more fully about my work on Zelen and what it was all about."

"Since your camera crew were going to give the game away anyhow," Claire reminded him.

"My camera crew had nothing to do with it," he answered coolly. "I fully intended to tell you sooner or later just what had brought me to Zelen. I'm sorry if my delay seems to you to have been devious."

"Don't worry, old chap," Jacques put in breezily. "It will all come out in the wash. Or, as we say in France, *Tout s'arrange*!" He held out his hand. "And thanks for a marvellous meal. If my wife is in a hurry to get home I'm sure you will understand it's because of her concern for her father. She doesn't like to leave him too long."

But Claire was not co-operating in her husband's effort to retrieve the situation. She gave Glyn a cool, "Goodbye, Mr Harney," and began to walk away.

"If you don't mind," Jennie called after her, "I'll come on a little later." The words astonished here even as she uttered them, but she could not leave things as they were—there were so many questions she wanted to ask, and at the back of her mind lurked the hope that the answer to some of them might solve the riddle of

Glyn Harney's contradictory behaviour. Was it guilt because of his deception that had made him decide there could never be any lasting friendship between them? Instinctively she knew he had been drawn to her. But instincts were frightening things : she did not always trust hers. They were too dangerous !

Claire's backward glance was vitriolic. "You do as you please !" she flung over her shoulder ill-temperedly.

Watching her go, Glyn shrugged. "Now you really have upset the applecart," he said as he resumed his seat at the terrace table, where Claire's after-dinner liqueur stood eloquently untouched in its crystal glass.

"You shouldn't have stayed with me, sweet Jennie. It will only make matters worse."

"I hoped it might make them better," Jennie said. "There's still so much I'm not clear about."

"Such as ?" Glyn probed, giving her an uneasy glance.

"Why you came to our house under false pretences? Why you didn't tell me the first time we met just who you were?"

He busied himself for a moment offering her a cigarette, lighting it for her.

"You haven't answered my questions," she reminded him when with these small activities completed he remained silent.

"There aren't any easy answers," he said at last, not meeting her steady, questioning look. "Maybe it was that I thought I might be more impressive to you as the wandering historian you took me for than as a T.V. hack, which, after all, is what I am, going hither and thither at the command of my bosses."

She took her head. "That wasn't the real reason."

"All right, if you want it spelled out it was simply that at that stage I wasn't telling anyone on Zelen just what my mission was. And when later you disclosed your Romaine identity I found it more than ever necessary to keep silent . . . fearing that you would refuse to have any more to do with me." His voice dropped as he added, "I might never have seen you again."

"But that," she reminded him, "was what you decided

would be wisest. You told me so that evening you waited for me and 'willed me to come to you' at the villa gate."

"Then you relayed your father's incredible invitation —asking me to visit him."

She was shocked at the naked opportunism implied in his words. "So the chance of meeting my father was more important to you than the unwisdom of continuing to meet me! Is that how it was?"

His dark blue eyes flashed despair. "Don't try to make me say things I shall regret, Jennie. Nothing in this crazy world is ever as simple or straightforward as your questions suggest. Let's leave it at that. I'm a complex character. Not worth your interest."

He stood up. "And now if you've finished your cigarette I'm going to put you in a taxi and send you home."

She felt a sharp pang of disappointment. What had she expected? That he would walk her home through the dark, thyme-scented woods, where they might speak again of the complications which beset them.

"What about that dance band you were so keen on?" she reminded him. The moment the words were out of her mouth she regretted she had spoken them. What was the matter with her tonight? Had she forgotten already Glyn's confession of his double-dealing? But as usual his presence seemed to rob her of all her common sense.

She saw his face grow stern. "I'm not dancing with you again tonight, my Jennie. You keep your dances for your fiancé."

He was perfectly right, of course. And she was in the wrong. Once more she had flung herself at him and once more she had been gently but firmly repulsed.

"Keep your dances for your fiancé." Had there been a hint of jealousy in the admonition? And if she could arouse his jealousy what deeper emotion could she evoke? Hurriedly she thrust this fruitless speculation away from her. What Glyn Harney might or might not feel about her could be of no importance to her. That was something she must never forget.

CHAPTER SEVEN

BUT it was no use. The more she tried to keep Glyn
Harney out of her mind the more he persisted in staying
there. In the silence of the night she lay in her bed,
fighting the turmoil of her thoughts. 'Keep your dances
for your fiancé,' he had bidden her. In less than twenty-
four hours John would be here with her. The reluctance
with which she faced this fact alarmed her. And close on
its heels came a revelation even more frightening.
Whatever feeling she might have, and must *not* have,
for Glyn Harney she was no longer in love with John.
Had she ever been? Not with the sort of love which
makes a marriage. Her contacts, however improbable,
with a stranger had wakened in her depths of emotion
she had never before experienced. Certainly not with
her childhood sweetheart. Her feeling for him, she
realised now, lying there in the summer darkness, had
been nothing more than an adolescent dream. So how
could she marry him? The answer obviously was that
she could not. The decision brought a sense of relief. A
decision, she suspected, which had been forming in the
back of her mind ever since his disturbing letter arrived.
She even tried to persuade herself that Glyn Harney had
nothing to do with it. If he had never existed she would
have found herself panic-stricken at the prospect of an
autumn wedding.

So now there would be no autumn wedding. It wasn't
going to be easy to tell John this when he arrived full of
his happy plans. Nervously she rehearsed little speeches;
tactful, apologetic, remorseful. But none of them
sounded convincing.

Somehow she got through the day which followed,
spending most of the time on the beach with Dimples
and her namnie.

Then it was Tuesday—Steamer Day. Getting up

early, she cast a hunted look out of the window at the panorama of wooded hills and inlets of blue sea. Sick with nerves, she ran down to the kitchen to collect her shopping list and drank the heartening cup of coffee Marie had prepared for her. This gave her a momentary illusion of courage, which quickly evaporated as she drove down the winding road to Modice. It was another sparkling day, all blue and golden. She would just have time to do her marketing before the steamer berthed. Already it was well above the horizon, and the sight of it was like a shouted challenge. In half an hour she would be face to face with John. What in heaven's name could she say to him? How would she start?

It came to her with a sense of reprieve that she couldn't very well spring her grave decision upon him the moment he set foot on shore after his long tiring journey. She would have to wait in all decency until he had had breakfast and a rest, though she couldn't quite imagine how she would behave during the awkward interval. Would she be able to conceal from him that something was seriously wrong?

Then it dawned on her that, of course, the first thing she would have to tell John was of her father's sudden illness. The worry occasioned by this would account, at least for the time, for anything odd in her manner.

She had reached the harbour now. Everything was heartlessly as usual, the cheery island women with their stalls of fruit and vegetables, the little pleasure boats swinging at anchor in the harbour basin. A trawler had just returned from a night's fishing and was unloading its silvery catch into baskets and boxes on the quayside.

The steamer came close inshore slowly, its propellors churning the water. Sailors shouted and threw ropes, gangways were dragged into position. Leaving her shopping in the parked car, Jennie walked over the cobbles to the water's edge. Now the hull of the steamer was a white wall, soaring above her. Forcing herself to look up at the passenger deck, she scanned the crowd surging towards the main gangway; mostly English visitors, she summed them up, no doubt bound for the Slavonia.

It was a moment or two, her heart dancing a nervous fandango, before she located John. There he was, smiling, and waving to her. In his eagerness he had seen her before she had seen him. Nice John! She had forgotten how nice he was, with his untidy tow-coloured hair and candid uncomplicated air. Not outstandingly handsome, nor specially tall—just his own familiar, dependable self. And he looked so happy. Her heart stopped its nervous fandango and dropped like a stone in her bosom. A cold heavy weight. How in heaven's name . . . oh, how, dear God, was she going to wipe that look of confident joy from off John's kind face? A face she had known and loved since she was nine years old. 'I'm going to marry John,' she had told herself then. And now she must keep saying to herself until she got used to it : "I am not going to marry John.' There must be no weakening, no compromise, but complete honesty, cold and sharp as a surgeon's knife—cutting away in one stroke the relationship they had built up between them.

She moved closer to the gangway. The holidaymakers were now hurrying down it, eager for the foreign land which awaited them. For the moment John was hidden from her view and when she found him again she saw with a start of surprise that he was not alone. His father, Sir Mark Davenham, was with him. It took her an instant to adjust herself to this unexpected development : Sir Mark arriving unannounced to share his son's Adriatic holiday! Well, why not? And in the event it was a welcome coincidence that the great heart specialist should have chosen this moment to make one of his rare visits to Zelen. It would be reassuring for her father to have his advice and opinion.

The gangway was still congested, John and his father waiting on the ship's deck, when Jennie saw Glyn Harney coming towards her. "Oh, no!" she murmured under her breath. "I can't bear it!" He came with his measured, arrogant tread to where she stood, his dark head held high, his eyes mocking her a little, but with a sort of affection too, enjoying the sight of her there on the quayside in her blue cotton frock, the sun on her bright hair.

"I'm not going to intrude on your meeting with your lover boy," he said, seeing the alarm in her glance. "I'm here to collect my camera team and take them to the Slavonia. I just wanted to tell you that I'm moving there. It will be more convenient if I'm under the same roof as my chaps."

"Of course!" she murmured in confusion. John and his father were coming down the gangway now, and Glyn Harney had tactfully melted away. The air was filled with cries of greeting as people on shore recognised friends on board. Sailors shouted, still busy with their ropes, while high overhead the luggage crane began its swinging journeys.

"Jennie! How marvellous!" John's arms were around her.

His kiss was wholehearted, if a little hurried; then Sir Mark gave her a friendly peck on the cheek. Dr Sinjek, he was explaining, had phoned him. "I didn't altogether like the sound of his report on your father; so I thought I'd pop over and see for myself how he really is."

It was good of him to have come, but she couldn't find the words of thanks she ought to have uttered, her heart full of sudden fear. "Our local doctor phoned you?" she exclaimed. "Does that mean my father is more ill than we suspected?"

"Don't look so alarmed, my dear," the great man rallied her. "It's simply that I thought we'd better play safe. After all, I know a great deal more about Adrian's constitution than this local doctor." Was his voice too smoothly reassuring?

They were walking towards the parked car now, Sir Mark's hand supporting her elbow, while John, a little way behind, coped with suitcases. She had lost sight of Glyn Harney, nor did she think of him and his camera crew, preoccupied with the disturbing implications of Sir Mark Davenham's unexpected appearance. She was wondering too what room they could give him. John would be quite happy in the attic Gervase had vacated, but the better guest rooms on the lower floor were all occupied. And Sir Mark wasn't just another of Adrian's bohemian friends with a blithe disregard for domestic comforts. He would expect all the amenities.

It was all a bit worrying, but it helped her through the difficult first half hour with John. She could meet his ardent gaze as he rejoined them without the awful sense of guilt sweeping over her. Emotional crises could wait.

"Did Father tell you," he was saying, "that we aren't going to impose ourselves on you at the villa when you have Adrian's illness to cope with? The travel gent who fixed our flight has booked us in at the Slavonia."

So Glyn Harney and John would be staying under the same roof!

"We'd better go there straight away, freshen up and rest a little," Sir Mark put in. "We won't disturb your father or your household at this unearthly hour . . . so if you could just drive us to the hotel, my dear. I understand it's quiet nearby."

Murmuring in a rather dazed tone that yes, it was, Jennie got into the driving seat. Sir Mark tucked himself into the rear of the car, while John sat by Jennie's side.

"It's so wonderful to see you, darling!" he said in a low tone as they set off. "Flying through the night to get to you, seeing the dawn over the Alps . . . I can't tell you how I've looked forward to this visit, though I know I mustn't be selfish and expect you to give me too much time. You'll be busy with your sick nursing. But can't you have dinner somewhere with me tonight . . . just the two of us? There's so much we have to talk about."

So much indeed! If only he knew! She felt mean and awful letting him think that most of her day would be taken up with looking after her father, not telling him they had a nurse. She could quite well have spared the time for a pre-lunch swim, or an afternoon of walking over the hills. But she seized on the hours of reprieve, hugging them to herself like a shield. Time enough this evening, she thought, to open her traitorous heart to him, wipe the shining happiness from his face. Dinner together would be lovely, she said. They could go out to Urbino, perhaps.

"Urbino will be heaven!" John breathed ecstatically. "Oh, Jennie darling, you do have the most wonderful ideas."

But she hardly heard him, sick with apprehension as they halted before the flamboyant portico of the big garish hotel. Supposing they ran into Glyn Harney and his camera team? He would be bound to acknowledge her. And Sir Mark would be curious. (She was picturing in her fevered fancy the cameraman rushing about the foyer already going into action with huge unwieldy cameras at the ready). But nothing dramatic happened. Glyn Harney was nowhere to be seen. And in any case she didn't have to penetrate the foyer, or even get out of the car.

"We'll see you later on, then, dear," Sir Mark was saying as he prepared to follow John and the suitcases through the great open glass doors. "I leave it to you to prepare your father for my unexpected arrival. He must on no account be alarmed by it. You must make it seem as if I'd decided upon a few days' holiday, acting on the spur of the moment because of the opportunity of travelling out with John."

"I'll see Father isn't upset," Jennie nodded. "There really isn't any reason why he should be. He'll be so pleased to see you that it will never occur to him to connect it with his illness—which he's taking very lightly."

"Good, good!" the great man boomed.

John put his hand on her shoulder in a gesture of farewell, smiling down at her, confidently, happily. "Tonight, my love!" he whispered. "Until tonight."

"But won't you both come up to lunch, when you've rested?" she felt impelled to suggest.

"I think not, my dear," Sir Mark replied. "It's very sweet of you. But I don't want to face your father until I'm completely refreshed. We will have an early lunch, catch up on some sleep and make our way to the Villa some time during the afternoon."

Speaking for John as well as himself, arranging

everything. But he was that sort of father, and John didn't seem to mind. Jennie's doubts as to the wisdom of this attitude must have showed in her expressive face. Surveying her, Sir Mark's smile was quizzical.

"Don't look so disappointed, my dear," he rallied her. "I know you and John have a lot to say to one another. I promise you that you'll have plenty of opportunity." The quizzical smile widened, became positively beatific. "We've always known, John's mother and I, the way you two felt about one another . . . and we're very glad. We couldn't wish for a more charming or lovable daughter-in-law."

Jennie suppressed a gasp of dismay. Sir Mark welcoming her into the Davenham family! But what a place to choose . . . standing beside the open car in the full glare of the Slavonia. And John looked so happy, stooping to give her a farewell kiss. Just what she said to them both she never knew, only that her cheeks were flaming as she started the car rather jerkily and drove away.

Somehow she was crossing the quay, making for the hill road. So it was all settled in the minds of the Davenham family! She felt as if a great sticky spider's web was being woven about her, snaring her.

They all take me for granted, she thought despairingly; John and his mother and father. The break was going to be more difficult than she had feared.

When she reached the Villa Claire and Jacques were having breakfast on the terrace, Dympna racing back and forth between them. As usual she was making a lot of noise. "It's just her way of realising herself," Claire explained with motherly pride. Jennie couldn't help wishing Dympna would go and realise herself somewhere else, as she shouted above the child's clamour in answer to Claire's shouted. "Where's John?"

"He's gone to the Slavonia, with his father."

"His father?" Claire exclaimed. "You mean Sir Mark has come to Zelen too?" But her words were almost drowned by her small daughter's rendering of her favourite, 'Three blind mice.'

"Dympna, be quiet!" Claire begged. But Dympna,

firmly launched on her song, went on in a high shrill key to relate the misfortunes of the sightless rodents.

"Dr Sinjek phoned him," Jennie shouted above the pandemonium, "perhaps asking for advice. Anyway, it rather alarmed Sir Mark and he decided to come along with John and have a look at Father. We have to tell him this without unduly worrying him, make it sound as if Sir Mark simply decided to have a few days' holiday on Zelen. And," she added, "they're staying at the Slavonia to save us trouble."

"I got just about half that," Claire wailed. "You'll have to tell it to me all over again when we've disposed of Dympna." She stood up and took her small daughter firmly by the hand, leading her into the house. "Nannie!" she called, "will you take Dympna now and get her ready for her morning on the beach?"

"No, no, *no*!" screamed Dympna, and the singing turned into a yell that would not have shamed a ship's siren. It grew louder and louder as Nannie led her away.

"Something will have to be done about that child," Jacques breathed darkly.

"Something *will* be done," Claire snapped. "She'll grow out of this phase if only we have patience and can interfere as little as possible. By the time she's five she'll be entirely different. Children have to go through these stages."

"By the time she's five we'll all be round the bend," Jacques declared inelegantly. Claire took no notice of him and turning to Jennie said, "Now please, Jen, begin again. Sir Mark is here with John. Where?"

"They're to stay at the Slavonia—at least while Sir Mark remains," Jennie began, and once more went through the story, enlarging this time on her own surprise when she saw Sir Mark coming down the gangway of the steamer. "He says we have to break the news of his visit to Father very carefully, and not alarm him."

"Is he himself alarmed...by Dr Sinjek's report?" Claire probed. They discussed the situation for some minutes, during which, to Jennie's relief, John was hardly mentioned.

"I'd better go and break the news of Sir Mark's arrival to Papa right away," Claire said presently. "I'll make it sound very casual."

Idling over her breakfast coffee and rolls, Jennie gazed unseeingly on the garden beyond the terrace, while Jacques talked about their morning plans, which need not be interfered with by the Davenhams' arrival. "We can drive over to the East Beach for our usual pre-lunch swim," he declared. But Jennie said she didn't think she had better go with him. "Dr Sinjek might be coming this morning," she offered on the spur of the moment. "And I'd like to ask him, if I get the chance, just why he sent for Sir Mark."

"Also there's this Harney character on the horizon," Jacques reminded her. "Isn't he supposed to be coming to collect some notes he left with Adrian?"

But just at that moment Claire returned to say that her father had taken the news of Sir Mark Davenham's visit very calmly. "In fact," she added, "he seemed relieved at the thought of consulting him. Maybe he's more concerned about his health than he let's us think," she ended with a worried sigh.

"What a shame John is going to be at the Slavonia," she said then, giving Jane a commiserating glance. "I'm afraid he won't have such a carefree holiday here as he usually does ... with this sickroom atmosphere intruding. You'll have to try to make it up to him, Jen. Did you ask him to come swimming with you this morning?"

"Sir Mark decided they ought to rest after their journey," Jennie answered. "And anyway, I'm not going swimming this morning."

"The villainous Harney is calling to collect some notes," Jacques put in with a mischievous grin at his young sister-in-law.

"Jennie doesn't have to forgo her swimming in order to receive him!" Claire snapped. She turned on her sister. "Just what is going on between you and that creep? Why did you stay behind with him when Jacques and I came home last night?"

"I didn't stay very long," Jennie pointed out, and

hated herself for sounding apologetic. "I merely wanted to ask him one or two questions about his work, and ease the situation a little, perhaps. You were pretty hard on him." If it wasn't the whole truth it would have to serve. "I wanted to make sure you hadn't made him feel he wasn't welcome to come and see Papa. I think his visits are important to Papa."

"And after all," Jacques joined in, "he has given us his word he won't say anything to upset our invalid. I don't see why you have to get so worked up about the chap, Claire."

"I don't like him," Claire said. "I did at first. He took me in with his smooth ways. Far too smooth! I might have guessed appearances were deceptive—something Jennie doesn't seem to have tumbled to yet. But it's all too obvious. The way he wormed his way into our confidence, keeping quiet about his TV connections. I think it's absolutely disgusting!"

"I know he acted deviously," Jennie admitted. "But that doesn't make him a criminal. He's just a TV journalist doing his job ... and I'm *not* staying at home to see *him*. I want to speak to Dr Sinjek if he turns up. Also the mail will be arriving from the steamer, and Papa will want me to read the English papers to him."

Even as she spoke the mail car stopped at the gate and getting out of it the postman was coming up the drive.

When the letters and packages had been sorted Jennie took her father's mail up to him, and for the next hour was busy helping him with his correspondence. She thought he seemed a little more languid than he had done yesterday, not really interested in his letters, and he didn't want the papers read to him just then. All his thoughts seemed to be centred on Glyn Harney.

"I would like to go through his notes on the cathedral again before he arrives," he said. So propping him up on his pillows Jennie laid the neatly typed pages on the bed table before him.

"It's wonderful," he mused, as he read, "the feeling this young man has for our cathedral and our beautiful

113

little city." And he began to read out in a soft voice the words which fell like poetry into the quietness of the shadowy sickroom. All the colours of the island were evoked, the jade green sea reflecting the pine trees and aloes and sword-like cacti leaning from the cliff walls to peer at themselves in the limpid depths. And above the golden bastion of the city walls the twin towers of the miniature cathedral rising, fragile as flower petals, against the sapphire sky : Glyn Harney had captured it all and written of it with love.

Later in the sanctuary of her own room Jennie found herself going over it all again in her mind, treasuring it. She was hearing her father say, "He writes like a painter, this boy. His awareness of colour and form, with their depth of meaning, is quite unusual. I've got to get out of this damned bed," he had added impatiently, "go down to the studio with him so that I can look at my cathedral abstract through his fresh vision."

And at any moment he would be walking up the drive, and she would have to escort him to the sickroom. This day . . . this strange day, Jennie thought in despair. How am I going to get through it? Glyn Harney and John staying at the same hotel. It was only a matter of time before she found herself introducing them to one another, a prospect which made her feel weak at the knees.

But in the end it was Marie who showed Glyn Harney up to the sickroom when he arrived, and Jennie did not see him until he was leaving. He came out of the house on to the terrace where she was writing a letter her father wanted sent off by the steamer when it returned to the mainland. He had suggested she might ask Glyn Harney to take it down to the port when he left. Claire and Jacques, after their swim, were idling over an aperitif. Glyn, seeing them, hesitated, as if he were not quite sure how Claire would greet him.

"Won't you join us for a drink, Mr Harney?" she said, with more cordiality than Jennie had expected. Perhaps Jacques had been talking sense into her. After all, if their father accepted the stranger and encouraged him to come to the house Claire could do no less without creating an embarrassing situation. At all events she actually smiled at him now as he thanked her and sat down in the wicker chair she indicated.

"How did you find the invalid today?" Jacques asked.

"Full of enthusiasm," Glyn returned. "He's hoping to persuade his doctor to allow him to go down to his studio for a little while, during the next day or two. Not to paint, of course, but he wants to talk to me about his abstract of your island cathedral."

His glance went to Jennie as he spoke. She bent her head over the letter she was writing, hurrying now to get it finished. From under the veil of hair which had flopped across her face she asked Glyn if he would post it for her. "It's an order for paints my father is sending to London, and he wants to get it off as quickly as possible."

He wouldn't be ordering quantities of fresh paints if he were really desperately ill, she told herself. His interest in his work was a good sign and it was Harney who had stimulated it. He likes Glyn, she thought, more than likes him. There seems to be a bond between them. Her heart warmed at the idea. Because she and her father had always shared so much—and now it seemed they both recognised in the stranger this special quality, this magnetism.

Of course he would be glad to post the letter, he was saying. Tossing her hair back over her shoulder, Jennie forced herself to meet his glance. Cool and assured it waited for her—those steady, disconcerting eyes; it was difficult to guess what was going on behind them, and yet they had an immediate power over her which she could not resist. Nor were they always so cool, so remote; she had seen them flame into passionate life.

Up the garden path at that moment came Dimples and her young nannie heralded by the flood of chatter which invariably announced the little girl's arrival. Mounting the terrace steps, she caught sight of Glyn Harney and flung herself at him with cries of delight. "Man! Man!" she chanted ecstatically, hugging him round the knees, gazing up at him with adoration. He stroked her golden curls. "Man!" she breathed in a besotted tone.

Adrian, Jennie thought wryly, and now Dimples... To say nothing of herself, caught by Glyn Harney's fatal charm!

But the moment of harmony was rudely interrupted. "Piggyback!" Dimples demanded. "Man give Dimples piggyback." She tugged at his arm with surprising strength.

"Not just now, sweetheart," Glyn protested. "I'm having a drink with your mummy and daddy."

"Piggyback! Piggyback!" Dympna yelled, and when Glyn ignored her she moved back a little, then running forward gave him a mighty kick on the shins. It must have hurt, but picking up his glass, Glyn remained studiously unmoved, making some remark to Jacques about the special quality of the island aperitif.

Enraged by this neglect, Dimples began to cry lustily, still screaming for her piggyback.

"*Stop it!*" Glyn suddenly shouted at her in a voice of thunder. "Stop that noise at once!"

Astonishingly, Dimples obeyed, gazing at him in blue-eyed surprise. "Stop it!" she echoed softly, experimentally, and then apparently liking the sound of the words repeated them again and again. "Stop it," she crooned, leaning against his knee. "Dimples like stop it."

Everyone laughed.

"She evidently approves of her man being the dominant male," Jacques said. "No Women's Lib for our Dimples!"

Glyn put an arm around the little girl's shoulder. She snuggled against him confidently. "Piggyback!" she suggested once more, but this time it was no more than a half apologetic whisper, while she continued to gaze up at him adoringly.

It was her lunch time, her mother interrupted a trifle sharply, not perhaps enjoying the sight of Dympna's infatuation for this tiresome stranger who seemed to be encroaching more and more into their family life. "Run along with Nannie now, darling," she admonished, and without a murmur or a word of protest Dimples complied.

"A miracle!" Jacques breathed in awe. "You have tamed our baby shrew, Harney. How did you do it?"

Glyn laughed. "Pure chance. Kids probably like a word of command now and again. Perhaps it gives them some kind of moral support. And maybe mine just now had effect because I'm somebody new."

"You seem to understand children pretty well," Jacques said admiringly.

"Perhaps you have a family of your own?" Claire probed.

Glyn seemed startled for an instant by the question before he answered with a shake of his dark head. "I'm afraid I'm not that lucky." And then, curtly, in a tone which discouraged further questions, "I'm not married."

He stood up, holding out his hand for the envelope Jennie was sealing.

"If I'm to get that letter on to the outgoing steamer I'd better be making tracks. And"—with a little bow in Claire's direction—"thanks for the drink."

He didn't meet Jennie's glance as he took the sealed envelope from her hand, and his back had an adamant look as he walked down the drive.

So he was not married, Jennie reflected. Somehow it had never seriously occurred to her that he might be. He had a footloose air.

CHAPTER EIGHT

JOHN and his father arrived at the villa soon after three o'clock that afternoon, to find Claire and Jennie resting on the terrace, leafing halfheartedly through magazines. There was a basket of sewing beside Claire, but she was too distraught to get on with the crochet work with which she often employed idle moments. And Jennie, gazing unseeingly at a fashion supplement, shared her mood. What would the great heart specialist have to say about their father's condition? The more they thought about it the more apprehensive they became. Surely it was something more than the casual medical report he had indicated which had uprooted him from his busy practice, his hospital commitments, and brought him hotfoot across Europe to this out-of-the-way island! He had already made it clear that he would have to return with the next mainland-bound steamer, so was obviously pressed for time.

Now when greetings had been exchanged—John gazing at Jennie with his heart in his eyes—both men went upstairs to the sickroom. They were gone what seemed an unconscionable time, Claire and Jennie growing more and more nervous, until at last in an attempt to occupy herself Claire had gone into the kitchen and prepared the tea trolley, ignoring Marie's disapproval of this intrusion into her duties.

"I've got to do *something* besides sit out there on the terrace and worry," she apologised to the old housekeeper. "I can't think what those two doctors are doing so long upstairs in my father's room."

"Having a nice chat, I shouldn't wonder," Marie offered consolingly. "After all, Sir Mark is an old friend of Monsieur's, as well as his medical adviser."

But at last approaching footsteps were heard. It was only Sir Mark who appeared. John, he said, had stayed behind to have a private talk with the patient. He shot a significant glance at Jennie as he spoke. Her heart sank. A private talk! Was it possible John was engaged in the archaic procedure of asking her father for 'her hand in marriage'?

"Ah, tea!" Sir Mark explained, eyeing the temptingly arrayed trolley appreciatively. "A cup will be very welcome." With a sigh of content he seated himself in one of the more comfortable of the wicker lounging chairs.

Claire's hand wielding the big silver teapot was not quite steady. "How did you find my father, Sir Mark?" she demanded abruptly, unable to wait a moment longer for the dreaded verdict.

Calmly the great man continued to enjoy his fragrant cup of tea. Surely he must realise how anxiously they were waiting for his report. Jacques had now joined them, but the three pairs of eyes, watching in agonised expectancy his every movement seemed to disturb Sir Mark not at all. When the last drop of tea had been disposed of he put down his cup, wiped his moustache, murmured, "Ah, that's better!" and looked smilingly around him. "Adrian is better than I thought to find him—from Sinjek's report." There was a perceptible lightening of the atmosphere around the tea table. "Which doesn't mean Sinjek in any way misled me. At the moment your father is a pretty sick man. But from what I can deduce from my somewhat superficial examination, his heart has not been too seriously damaged by this attack he has had. I propose to borrow some equipment from the local hospital, with Sinjek's cooperation, and then I shall be able to go into the matter more thoroughly. I didn't ask Sinjek to meet me here this afternoon as we didn't want Adrian to realise we had been in touch. It would only have alarmed him. I'm seeing him presently in his own surgery. Meanwhile I've prescribed some simple remedies for Adrian and told him he must rest."

"Are you telling us that we needn't be unduly anxious about our father?" Claire ventured.

Sir Mark pondered. "I wouldn't quite put it like

that," he began cautiously. "There's always cause for some anxiety in cases of this sort. But providing Adrian follows my advice and rests for a week or so all should be well. And when I say rest I mean rest of mind and soul as well as body. He must on no account be emotionally disturbed, nor crossed, nor frustrated, even in the smallest matters. Give in to him in every way possible. Give him all he wants within reason . . . and no arguments." The old man nodded pontifically.

"For instance," he went on, "he says he must get down to his studio in the garden to discuss some magnum opus which is the light of his eye with an expert on these matters who happens to be visiting Zelen. It's out of the question for him to walk to his studio, so I'm going to arrange for a wheelchair to be sent up from the hospital, with the rest of the equipment I'm hoping they will provide."

He nodded at the eagerly listening Claire. "Just humour your father in every way," he ended.

Claire gave a great sigh of relief. Even with its reservations, Sir Mark's verdict was much better than she had dared to hope. In her wildest moments of optimism she wouldn't have imagined the patient being allowed to go down to the studio—even in a wheelchair.

"Luckily he has a fairly equable temperament," Sir Mark was saying then. "But like most people of that type if he *is* roused or upset it goes pretty deeply."

"He won't be upset," Claire pronounced firmly. "We'll all see to that, and anyway there's nothing I know of at the moment that could possibly worry him. Do you think he'll be all right for the journey back to London in the autumn?"

"Oh, good lord, yes!" Sir Mark boomed. And just then John came out of the house, looking beatific. Pulling a chair up beside Jennie, he placed a proprietorial hand on her arm, his grey eyes giving her an adoring and specially significant glance.

"It's all sewn up!" Jennie thought despairingly. "Papa and John have been arranging the wedding between them, taking the situation for granted." Maybe that wasn't so extraordinary. Even if she and John hadn't been engaged they had been close friends for the last three years—in a rather special way. And Adrian had always had a soft spot for John. Now that he was a qualified M.D. he would be in a position to marry. So it was natural enough, Jennie supposed, for him to have been discussing it with her father this afternoon. In fact everything about the situation was completely natural and normal . . . save her own sudden and total change of heart.

Once more she wondered how she was going to disentangle herself. Had her father really set his heart upon her marrying John? Thinking back at various hints he had dropped there was evidence that he had. How would he take it if he were to be told now that the marriage had become impossible because of his daughter's defection?

"There must be no arguments," Sir Mark had ordered. The invalid must be humoured in every way. That is, if they were going to help him towards a complete recovery from his heart attack. His peace of mind was all-important.

What, Jennie wondered desperately, was she going to do?

When presently she slipped upstairs to the sickroom her worst forebodings were realised. Adrian, sitting in a chair by the window, greeted her with obviously special tenderness. "Darling Jennie!" he began, motioning her to a chair beside his own, "John tells me he's taking you out to Urbino this evening for dinner. That will be nice for you . . . getting away from the rest of us for the time together you must be longing for. You mustn't let my being a bit off colour spoil your days while John is here."

"Of course it won't spoil our days," Jennie put in vigorously. "Nothing on earth would prevent me being with you just now when you need me. . . ."

He held up a silencing hand. "Sweet child, I don't expect you to neglect John on my account. It's a very special time for you. He and I have been having a little chat and I'm so glad you've decided that your marriage is to be fairly soon."

But we haven't decided anything of the kind, Jennie longed to interject. At least *I* haven't decided—since my opinion hasn't yet been discussed.

She left the disturbing words unspoken, and took the hand her father held out to her. "It's especially important to me just now to feel your future is settled," he was saying. The fingers holding her own were, she noticed, icy cold, in spite of the heat of the afternoon. "It will be a relief to me to see you safely married to dear John. He's a good boy and will take care of you. I shan't be here with you indefinitely . . . that's a fact we must all face."

Jennie's heart sank. "But you're rapidly getting better. Sir Mark says so."

"I know," her father nodded. "And the broken gate hangs on its hinges the longest. But the time will inevitably come when in the nature of things I must leave you all."

"But not for years," Jennie declared emphatically.

Her father gave her hand a little squeeze. "The more years the better. There's still so much I want to do; besides wearing my best grey top hat and white gardenia in my buttonhole at your wedding." He gave her a twinkling smile. "John tells me he's going to get cracking organising all the details as soon as he gets back to town; that's when you and he have decided just what kind of wedding you want. I imagine it will be a white one—with all the frills, and Lady Davenham very much in evidence!" His little spurt of laughter held affection and tolerance. Lady Davenham was notoriously a 'manager' where her two menfolk were concerned. "But we mustn't let her have it all her own way. We must write and tell your mother the news as soon as possible, find out when she's coming home."

All this was altogether too much for poor Jennie. Swallowing a lump in her throat, she said, "But, Pops darling, you're going too fast! I haven't had the chance of talking to John about it yet. We can sort it out when we go Urbino presently."

"Sort it out?" her father murmured a little doubtfully.

"I mean find out how we both feel about it," Jennie blundered.

"Do you mean there's any question?" Adrian sounded disturbed.

No arguments, no discussions, Sir Mark had said. No emotional upsets.

"Of course not," Jennie returned vigorously. "It's just that we've hardly had the chance to even say hullo to one another yet." She laughed shakily and Adrian, releasing her hand, shook his head remorsefully. "I'm a selfish old man, and a complete nuisance into the bargain. Having heart attacks and making myself the centre of attention at this special time which should be all yours."

Jennie flung impetuous arms around his neck. "It's perfectly right that you should be the centre of attention, darling. You'll always be the centre of *my* attention no matter how many husbands I may marry!"

At which they both laughed and the atmosphere cleared.

The whole world was rosy with sunset light when later Jennie and John drove up the winding roads to Urbino. On their right the pinewoods were dense, clothing a steep hillside, while on the left the stony fields with their stunted olive groves swept down to the sea. Jennie, at the wheel of the car, made a show of being engrossed in the business of driving. Since they left the villa they had exchanged only platitudes—and that wasn't going to satisfy John for long. When it came to the crunch what on earth was she going to say to him? With an honesty which was almost naïve she was no good at subtleties, or subterfuge. But the unpalatable truths she had seen herself being forced to offer were now impossible. So what? She must for the moment go along with the situation as it existed . . . for Adrian's sake.

"Can't we pull up a minute?" John was demanding presently. "Here in this layby with its glorious view of the coast."

But Jennie knew it wasn't coastline views that really interested him, and no sooner had she switched off the engine than his arms were about her. Drawing her gently towards him, he looked into her face enquiringly. "What is it, Jen?" he asked. "I've felt you so far away from me ever since I arrived. Is it that you're worried about your father?"

A suggestion she seized on. "Of course I'm worried, and even though Sir Mark is going out of his way to be reassuring I don't feel wholly convinced. What do *you* think of Papa . . . honestly, John?"

"I can't add anything to what my father has told you," John returned loyally. "If he spoke to you reassuringly, then you may *be* assured. He's not in the habit of making false reports to his patients' families. . . ."

"I didn't mean to imply that," Jennie put in hurriedly, her tactlessness adding to her sense of guilt. "I only wanted to get *your* opinion."

"Worth a good deal less than my father's," he reminded her. "But personally I was agreeably surprised to find Adrian no worse than he is."

"And what exactly does that mean?"

John mused a moment. "Well, he's a man in his late sixties who has, I understand, been making heavy demands upon his constitution . . . working on an outsize canvas for hours at a stretch. He stands at the top of a ladder, he tells us, often having to reach up, and all the time holding a heavy palette. He would have to have the strength of a young professional housepainter to keep it up. The miracle is that he hasn't done himself more harm. But he has remarkable recuperative powers. If he eases off now and leads the kind of life more suitable to his age he should live for years. Fortunately this immense painting of the cathedral which has been occupying him is, he says, just about complete, and he has promised, under duress, to leave it now as it is."

He drew her closer. "Does that make you feel happier, sweetheart?"

"Yes, of course," but her tone was still a little uncertain.

"He's delighted about us," John went on.

Jennie said nothing. It was an odd silence, eloquent of unease.

John gave her a baffled glance. "Jennie, what *is* the matter?" he burst out. "You got my letter, didn't you?"

"Yes, I got your letter." She lifted imploring eyes to him and was horrified to feel tears gathering. They rolled down her cheeks, her breath caught in her throat and the next moment she was sobbing in John's arms.

"Dear love," he soothed her, "you've been having a hell of a time. I wasn't to realise what you were going through with your father when I wrote to you of my lighthearted plans."

His shoulder was broad, his hand stroking her hair infinitely gentle. I shouldn't be taking comfort from him like this, her conscience pricked her. But the warmth and strength of his hard young body seemed to flow into her. It was good to cry, he told her. It would relieve the tensions she had obviously been bottling up for the past few days.

"We won't talk about weddings until you are feeling better," he promised.

Once more guilt engulfed her. "It's just, I think, that I wasn't quite ready for it. Even apart from my worry about Papa," she offered in honesty, moving away from him a little, wiping her eyes on the large handkerchief John had produced. "I mean," she faltered, "we've drifted along in our vaguely happy way for years . . . and suddenly everything was different."

She could not explain *how* different! And John thought she was referring to the general upheaval to her way of life which marriage would inevitably bring.

He said, "I've been a clumsy fool, darling, sending you that bombshell of a letter. But of course I had no idea your father was going to have this alarming heart attack. I was so thrilled about the flat my father is giving us and so forth . . . the prospect of working with him when I've got my consultancy." He drew her close to him again. "And having you with me for keeps . . . in our own home. Oh, Jen, just think of it!"

"I know," she agreed in a small voice. "It's all very wonderful, but what with one thing and another this week it was a bit much for me to take in."

If only he knew what that 'one thing and another' covered! She longed to tell him. But because of her father's illness she could not. There must be no denial of their engagement at this stage, no emotional rift between the two families. She could only drift on, playing for time, hoping things would somehow, in some way, sort themselves out—a pretty thin consolation, but it was all she had.

With a last puzzled look at her wan, distraught face John said, "Well, we must leave it all for the moment, love. Talk about it when you're feeling more rested. Right now I'm going to take the wheel and drive you to Urbino. What you need more than anything at this point is a dish of Stefano's excellent kebab and a glass of his *ružica*."

There was a holiday air when they drove presently along the village street. Tonight most of the young girls and women were wearing colourful national costumes, the young men resplendent in knee-breeches and feathered hats. Dancing had already begun, the air shrill with the music of the fiddlers. Stefano came out of the inn to greet them when, having parked the car, they strolled towards the long scrubbed table under the overhanging eaves.

"The young Mr Davenham!" he hailed John with warm recognition. "You have come back to Zelen. You cannot keep away from us, is it not so?"

"Indeed it is," John agreed, his arm about Jennie's shoulder. "And you've put on a special show for us, I see. Is it some kind of festival tonight?"

Stefano, ushering them to a place at the communal table, said no, it was not a festival. "Some Englishmen with cameras who are going to make a film for television came here this morning asking if the villagers would be willing to do a few traditional dances for them. Tonight they are rehearsing." He turned to Jennie. "It was your friend the Gospodin Harney who brought these cameramen and arranged it all."

"Oh, yes, Mr Harney," Jennie said hurriedly, as if she were trying to remember just who he was.

"Your father spoke of him this morning," John put in. "It seems he is some kind of Balkan historian. But Adrian didn't say anything about him being in any way connected with television. I thought your father hid himself on Zelen mainly to escape from such people, with their prying cameras and inquisitive minds. Yet this Harney type," ended John, sounding puzzled, "has actually been admitted to the villa."

"Papa doesn't know he has anything to do with television," Jennie said, feeling more and more uncomfortable. "Nor is there any need for him to know. Glyn Harney isn't going to include anything about him or his work on this film he's making. He's promised us this. And meanwhile Papa likes talking to him about the island and the cathedral and so on, because Glyn Harney is something of an expert on Mediterranean islands and Balkan affairs. It just came about by chance . . . our getting to know him," she finished lamely, and was saved from further explanations by Stefano pouring glasses of *ružica* for them and asking what they would like to have for dinner. A lengthy discussion on the menu followed.

Taking a gulp of *ružica*, Jennie wondered nervously where the conversation would lead next. Somehow she had got to keep it away from Glyn Harney. Though why she couldn't simply have told John how she had met the young man accidently, and later brought him to Urbino because he asked her where he could find traditional dancers, she couldn't have said. The very mentioning of his name filled her with anxiety . . . and guilt.

Luckily Stefano's attentiveness and the noise of the music and dancing did not make sustained conversation easy—nor did John seem interested in asking any more questions about Glyn Harney. He was absorbed in watching the colourful performance under the pepper trees on the dramatically illuminated square, special floodlighting have been produced this evening. Obviously it was in every way a full dress rehearsal for the distinction of appearing in a TV film.

Round and round circled the dancers, the same hypnotic melody repeated again and again. The voluminous skirts of the women flared about them as they spun with their partners. Quicker and quicker went the music, faster and faster the dancers followed it. Now and then a male dancer would utter a wild cry as the *kolo* progressed, the unbroken ring circling first in one direction and then in another, clockwise and anti-clockwise; with the stamping of feet and hoarse cries to mark the rhythm. No hands were put out this evening to invite the visitors into the ring. The moment was too serious for such frivolous interruption. But Jennie was remembering how she and Glyn had joined in the dance the other evening, breathless and laughing.

It was a pity it wasn't the kind of dancing they could have taken part in, John remarked a little wistfully presently. "Perhaps if we went back to the Slavonia we could dance there," he suggested. "They seem to have a super ballroom and no doubt a dance band to match."

But Jennie said she was too tired for dancing this evening and if he didn't mind she would like to go home.

If he was disappointed at the early ending of their evening he did not say so. Jennie's weary look was not lost on his professional eye. He put it down to her anxiety about her father. Tomorrow, when she had had a good night's rest, she would be more like her old self.

Once more he insisted upon driving, and it was when they were about half way home that he stopped the car. At the very spot where Jennie herself had halted the night she and Glyn were returning from Urbino. It was the obvious pull-up, of course, a widening curve in the road making a natural lay-by overlooking the superb panorama of sea and sky and coastline. Far below they could see the lights of Modice reflected in the harbour basin. In the dusky summer night, which would never be quite dark, the effect was very beautiful. The sudden silence which fell on them as the engine was switched off added the final hint of the romantic. And of course the inevitable happened. Here on this spot where Glyn had kissed her, John leaned over her and took her in his arms. But his kiss was not like Glyn's kiss; gentle, almost diffident, a questioning kiss, probing her heart, leaving it melted in her breast. There had been tenderness in that kiss, while John's embrace was young and hot and impatient.

"Oh, Jennie!" he sighed. "I want you so much, my darling."

If she was unresponsive he didn't seem to notice it, kissing her again and again until at last he was reproaching himself, saying he had forgotten how tired she was. He would take her home at once. "I must learn to take care of you, my little love," he said, swinging the car out on the road, sending it speeding through the scented starlit night, down through the pinewoods and the sad stony fields until they reached the villa.

When at last she found herself in her own room the relief of being alone was so great that she was almost happy. The long agonising day was over. And what a day! Like a reel unwinding its events flashed before her. Waiting on the quayside for the steamer to arrive, seeing John waving to her from the deck, the shock of Sir Mark's unexpected appearance and all the subsequent suspense about her father's heart condition. The strain all day of trying to act naturally with John in front of the family, and the immeasurably greater strain of their evening together. His kisses had left her cold, even faintly repelled. If she had hoped for anything from their meeting that hope must now be abandoned. All that had existed between them, the vague romantic dreams, had been a warm sweet part of her childhood. But when Glyn Harney walked into her life childhood had been left behind. It was as if he had called to her and she had come out of her small and sheltered world into a wide and shining place, filled with a beauty which made her tremble. She had crossed a boundary and she could never turn back. Yet the plans for her marriage to John must at least appear to go ahead—for her father's sake. He must not be thwarted in this matter which unfortunately seemed to be of vital importance to him.

The wheelchair arrived from the hospital the following day. Jennie was taking her father in it to the studio when she saw Glyn Harney coming up the garden driveway towards them. He was good to look at in his carelessly worn beach clothes; the gaily coloured shirt and trimly cut linen slacks. Cool, assured, wholly self-possessed, he approached them, his eyes holding no special message for Jennie as he greeted them. She dropped her own before his impersonal but probing glance, remembering the strange thing he had said to her when she had first shown him the studio. That odd gesture, tracing the outlines of her face with a fingertip, closing her eyes gently and saying, "It's easier when I don't see your eyes." Was it because of the unguarded light in them, the unconscious appeal? If only she did not feel so helpless before this man!

Adrian, hailing him with enthusiasm, made brave little jokes about the wheelchair, and Glyn put a hand close to Jennie's, helping her to push it the last few yards to the studio. Once when their hands touched he drew his own quickly aside. Had he felt the small contact as electrically disturbing as she had? He's not indifferent to me, she thought. However improbable and impossible it might be, there was a bond between them. She was sure of it at that moment

But once inside the studio it was as if the two men had completely forgotten her existence. Confronted by the immense canvas, they remained for a time in silence before it. Then Adrian, moving his wheelchair closer, began to talk rapidly, brilliantly of the different levels of the composition, each level with its own significance.

"In every brush stroke I've tried to evoke the love and courage which went into the building of our little cathedral. It's not simply made of wood and marble and stone and precious metals, but of the lives of the people of the island."

"It's that which gives it its extraordinary appeal," Glyn said.

"I've tried to achieve in it an added dimension, a spiritual appeal. Though it's not representative in the narrow sense it has a story to tell, a history to record. Much of my own experience has gone into it, as well as the experiences of the people of Zelen. It's the universality of human courage and suffering, of loving and living I've tried to immortalise. 'The apple tree, the singing, and the gold'."

"Is that to be its title?" Glyn asked, sounding a trifle puzzled.

"I don't know," Adrian admitted. "It's a little clumsy as a title. It's a line from a poem I read somewhere. If I had ever had the energy to write my memoirs I would, I think, have divided it into those three periods. The apple tree with its blossom for spring time and youth. The singing for creativity; the years of work, of childbearing, of achievement. And finally the gold of harvest, the quiet last years, mellow with fruit and fulfilment."

"If life could really be like that," Glyn said softly, and meeting his glance at that moment Jennie saw pain in its depths.

Adrian, however, ignoring the interruption with the egotism of the old, was saying that the poetic line almost gave him the courage to do something about those memoirs. "But I shall never get down to it. I'm too lazy and," he gave a deep sigh, "it's too late. I've put all I have felt into this painting instead—and it must stand as my record."

"Perhaps it will be even more adequate than the written word," Glyn suggested. "It's rapidly becoming a world of visual communication, rather than literary. People are increasingly disinclined to read great tomes of memoirs."

"Then you think my painting may have a wider appeal than a book?" Adrian asked.

"For those who are lucky enough to see it."

Adrian pondered this reply a moment and then said: "I've thought about that aspect of it, wondering how I could make sure the largest number of people would have access to it. So I've decided to leave it to the National Gallery," he announced. "But even there, how many people will go and look at it? I wish I could show it to the whole world—not because I'm a megalomaniac, but because I believe that with its record of this brave and beautiful island it contains some of the eternal truth."

He mused for a moment and then went on a little uncertainly: "Perhaps if it were to be broken up into a series of sectional photographs, to be exhibited with spoken explanations." He laughed. "It's beginning to sound like some enterprise on a television screen, but indeed it's the kind of thing that has been successfully done once or twice on television. I'm thinking of Sir Kenneth Clark's series, called, I believe, 'Civilisation'."

Listening to all this, Jennie could hardly believe her ears.

"But a television production, *and* in the right sort of colour, would be perfectly possible," she heard Glyn confirm. "Your painting could be shown first as a whole, and then broken up into the sections you suggest, accompanied by an appropriate commentary." He waved a hand at the great canvas, and warming to his theme went on: "Those distant figures seen through your interpretation of the cathedral windows—broken, but because of that all the more revealing. Like the enrichment of life which sometimes comes from a broken heart."

For a moment he was silent.

"Go on!" Adrian urged. "I'm caught up in your vision."

"The hints of battles fought and won," Glyn continued, "children playing on the edge of battlefields, the strange creatures, half bird, half human, with their

Blakesian symbolism ... the immortal phoenix rising from the ashes of human hopes. All this. ..." He broke off with a wave of his hand, as if words failed him.

Jennie heard her father draw in a quick breath. "If my painting really could be seen and understood like that. My painting ... and your words! But who could arrange it?"

"I could," Glyn said quietly.

In the weighted pause which followed Jennie sent him an appealing glance, longing to cry out to him in warning. Surely he was not going to disclose his identity as a television writer! She clenched her hands as if to hold back the reaction that must inevitably come. If her father realised he had been tricked into receiving a television operator, talking to him, opening his heart to him, confiding in him—surely his anger would be uncontrollable. And anger of that magnitude could kill him!

But quite calmly he was saying, "You mean you could introduce me to some of these television magnates?"

"I certainly could," Glyn confirmed with an easy laugh. "As it happens I work for them. It's for a television network I'm doing this survey of Zelen—though I hadn't dreamed of being able to include in it anything so stupendous as the magnum opus of Adrian Romaine."

Jennie closed her eyes, waiting for the storm to burst, but to her astonishment she heard her father say, "What a remarkable coincidence! If in the past I've distrusted all journalists and reporters with their fatuous commentaries it was because I'd never met anyone like you. Perhaps you are unique. But your perceptiveness about my work, your sensitivity and rare understanding of its meaning, makes me glad to accept your help."

CHAPTER NINE

CLAIRE'S reaction to Jennie's account of the morning's developments in the studio was one of indignation and alarm. They were having a pre-lunch aperitif on the terrace; Claire and Jacques and John, when Jennie joined them, Adrian having been safely delivered back to his sickroom. Glyn had gone off to his hotel straight from the studio.

"He broke his word to us," Claire stormed. "Blurting out his TV connection in a way which might have upset Papa terribly!"

"But it didn't," Jacques reminded her equably, as usual pouring oil on the troubled waters. But Claire was not to be appeased.

"Harney took a serious risk, and it's no thanks to him that it came off. He's an unscrupulous opportunist, making use of everyone he comes across. All he cares about is his personal success. And getting the elusive Romaine into his net must be a terrific triumph for him—the TV scoop of the year. He'll be on Papa's trail for weeks now, probably even after Papa gets back to London. Important commentaries on subjects like the Romaine paintings aren't disposed of in a few days. That man is going to stick like a limpet."

"He seems a decent enough chap," John put in mildly. "I've met him briefly at the hotel. As it happens we had breakfast with him this morning. My old man quite liked him."

"Everyone likes him," snapped Claire. "He sees to it that they do!" And after a moment, "I should have thought the Slavonia was large enough to provide its various guests with separate breakfast tables."

John laughed. "Of course it is. But you know what my father is—or perhaps you don't. When he's in holiday mood, or travelling, he talks to everybody. And Harney was responsive."

"I bet he was!" Claire sneered.

A few minutes later she and Jacques withdrew, rather ostentatiously leaving the lovers together.

John quickly moved his chair close to Jennie's, gazing at her in adoration. The green and gold light flickering through the overhead vine leaves danced on his tow-coloured hair and pleasant young face. The look of complete happiness on it smote Jennie's heart.

"It hasn't been much of a morning, has it?" he said wistfully. "You closeted with your father in the studio while I put in the time swimming with Claire and Jacques. And this afternoon is going to be no better. Sinjek is joining us in the sickroom for a consultation, and some further examination of your father's condition, with the help of the equipment we've borrowed from the hospital." He made a rueful grimace. "Your father won't like it, but its got to be done. And when we're through," he shrugged, "my time for what's left of the day will be my own . . . and yours, darling. What about dinner at the Slavonia . . . and a spot of dancing? I feel we both need cheering up and it seems a fairly cheery joint. Good floor, good orchestra and of course good food. What do you say?"

There was nothing for Jennie but a show of warm agreement. John liked dancing and was adept at it.

"Built with the Mediterranean spread at its foot, the ancient walled town of Modice at its back, the Slavonia enjoys one of the most beautiful prospects on the Adriatic," she murmured.

"You sound like a brochure," John told her.

"It *is* from a brochure." She gazed out over the sun-drenched garden, remembering that Glyn Harney had quoted it to her that morning they had looked down on the hotel and its panorama from the Cathedral place—the day Glyn had chosen to live at the humble *kafana*. But the camera crew had changed all that. Would she see him at the Slavonia tonight? Would he perhaps ask her to dance? He was already on friendly terms with the easy-going John, it seemed. She thrust the traitorous speculation away from her.

"What about your father this evening?" she asked, with a vision of the gregarious old man and a dinner table shared with an interesting stranger.

"Oh, he'll have the sense to keep out of our way," John assured her. "I expect he'll dine here with your sister and her husband, if they're kind enough to invite him. In that way he could spend a little time with your father."

And that, in the event, was how it turned out.

Later as Jennie dressed for the evening, she found herself taking special pains to be sure she would look her best. The frock she chose was a glamorous little number she had hardly yet worn, long-skirted, soft and frilly, full of feminine appeal. And it wasn't until she was putting the final dabs of scent behind her ears that she realised with her inconvenient habit of inner honesty that it wasn't for John she was taking all this trouble. The possibility of a dance with Glyn continued to lurk, or even a friendly aperitif with him before the meal, now that John was on friendly terms with him. It was no use being angry with herself for these straying thoughts; there was nothing she could do about them. The prospect of an encounter with Glyn in the romantic setting of the Slavonia's white and gold ballroom continued to obsess her. And it was useless to try to shame herself out of it.

John called for her about seven, apologising for the fact that he hadn't yet had time to change. He had been kept busy by his father, first there was the long consultation with Dr Sinjek and then Sir Mark wanted him to make very full notes of the consultation and of all their investigations into Adrian Romaine's condition.

"I hope you don't mind waiting for me, darling?" he said when they reached the foyer of the hotel. "I'll have to put on full evening togs if I'm to be fit to be your escort in that gorgeous dress—but I'll be as quick as I can."

"I'll be all right here," Jennie smiled up at him, finding herself a corner on a capacious settee flanked by a small table on which were some magazines. Leafing through the pages of a highly coloured fashion number, she found herself watching the swing doors of the entry, or glancing in the direction of a terrace bar near by. She could see the lifts too, not very far off, flanked by potted palms. Sooner or later, she felt certain, Glyn would appear. He would have to. She was conscious of so strange a sense of expectancy.

It was not, however, Glyn who answered these expectations but a pair of long-haired, rather raffish-looking young men, carrying compact if complicated photographic apparatus. Glyn Harney's camera team! They looked slightly weary, but exultant, as if they had had a good day, taking the sort of pictures they wanted. As they threw themselves down in a couple of deep chairs just behind Jennie's settee, she heard them summon a waiter and order drinks.

"This island . . . it's a natural," one of the young men begun. "That place up by the cathedral with the gorgeous gypsy type in a ragged velvet jacket whirring his knife machine under a fig tree, the women gathered around him, laughing, gossiping. It's almost too contrived to be real, save for the superb light and colour."

"And that extraordinarily beautiful toy cathedral in the background," contributed voice number two.

"Where's Harney, I wonder?" his companion put in.

"He was waiting for a London call. I expect it's come through, and he'll be having a whale of a time relating his triumphs. Old man Romaine in the bag. Whoever would have thought it! But Harney always did have the devil's own luck. Especially with women."

"Think of it!" mused voice number one. "The moment the steamer touched berth the other day there she was, Romaine's lovely daughter, and our Glyn gazing down at her wondering how he'd get himself across to her."

"How did he work it, in fact?" breathed voice number two. There was a pause while the waiter served their drinks and they sampled them, with a murmur of 'Cheers!'

"Talk about contrived!" exclaimed voice number one. "The coincidence to end all romantic coincidences. It seems a crane swinging out from the ship's side brushed the little darling's shoulder, almost knocking her into the harbour. But the hero Harney is on hand, puts a knightly arm about her and takes her to the nearest café for a reviving drink. After that, of course, it was all plain sailing. Whatever he said to that dame the magic worked and before you could say Jack Robinson she'd invited him up to the villa where they live to meet her father."

"But I thought old Romaine absolutely refused to receive press men or television types?"

"Don't be so naïve, Mike! Do you imagine Harney told the daughter, or her father, that he was in any way connected with the mass media? Oh, no, boy! Our wily friend passed himself off as a Balkan historian, if you please, said he was writing a book on Zelen's troubled past." There was a spurt of laughter. "Then coincidence number two comes along. Harney gets all steamed up about the miniature cathedral—genuinely enough—and it so happens ... wait for it! ... Romaine is doing what he considers to be the greatest painting of his life ... the subject, the cathedral. Apparently it's a mammoth abstract, and Harney, when the moment was ripe, managed to mesmerise the old man into deciding a series on television next winter would be the best way of introducing this magnum opus to a waiting world."

"Good lord!" groaned the one who had been called Mike. "What a saga! When did Harney tell you all this?"

"Last night after you'd gone to bed. We'd had rather a large number of noggins of the local slivovitch ... plum brandy to you ... and the boy was more talkative than usual. Not that he told me the tale quite in the way I've relayed it to you. His account was much more in keeping with his dignity—but I've filled in the spicy bits for you."

"And tomorrow," mused Mike, "we go up to the villa and start taking pictures of the masterpiece! I still can't believe it. Harney the golden boy, darling of the network! What say we go and rout him out of the office or wherever he is and buy him a drink? He must be finished sending his success story, his all-time scoop, to London by now."

Jennie, with what was left of her shattered consciousness, was aware of the sounds of their departure from their chairs behind the settee. She did not turn her head to look after them. She felt stiff and rigid all over, as if she would never be able to move again, and her eyes were closed, shutting her in with her black despair. Glyn Harney had recognised her that morning as she stood on the quayside waiting for the steamer to berth. And every word he had spoken to her since that moment had been an insult . . . and a lie. Fool, fool that she had been!

But she could not yet quite take it in. Shock stupefied her. When John returned presently, apologising for being so long, she laughed at him in an odd reckless way, telling him it did not matter. "You might have been away ten minutes or a hundred years," she told him. "I feel as if I'd been on a journey to outer space! I think I must have dozed off for a moment or two, and had the most extraordinary dream. A sort of nightmare!" She shuddered as she spoke.

John was instantly all concern. "Darling, you must be more tired than you admit, to doze off like that! Are you sure you're all right? Would you rather I took you home for a quiet meal and an early night?"

"After all the trouble I've taken making myself look trendy for the Slavonia! And for you" she added as a rather obvious afterthought. "Oh, no, John dear, I'm perfectly okay. It's just sun and sea, I expect. I spent most of the afternoon on the beach with Dimples and Nannie while you and Sir Mark were with Father. All I want now is a nice cold drink with lots of ice in it and I'll be as right as rain, ready for that gorgeous meal you promised me, and the dancing afterwards."

He took her out on to the terrace bar, clear as she knew it would be of Glyn Harney and his camera boys, for they had gone off into the interior of the hotel in their search for him, where they would probably have ended up in the smoking room bar, a haunt almost exclusively masculine. She had two Camparis, which increased her sense of heady unreality, carrying her through the lengthy ritual of dinner, during which she heard herself chattering with unnatural loquaciousness. After the meal they danced, but very soon dancing wasn't enough for John and he took her out through the floodlit garden to the white curve of sand which was the Slavonia's private beach. Here there were no lights save the phosphorescent gleam of the sea and the glitter of the stars. The moon, which was rising later now, had not yet appeared, so the night was full of shadows and the faint whispering of trees. Inevitably John took her in his arms and began kissing her. Once more he was telling her he loved her, wanted her. "You're so beautiful, so sweet!" he whispered, kissing her lips, her closed eyelids, the tip of one ear. "I can't think of anything more wonderful than to spend the rest of my life looking after you taking care of you, making you happy."

Something stirred in her frozen heart, a pain that was not made of sorrow or self-pity, but of a sharpened awareness. She could feel John's goodness, his integrity, his simple devotion. It was gratitude and a sense of her own unworthiness which this time brought the tears to her eyes.

John held her away from him a little. "Oh, my love, what is it?" he asked. "Why do you always weep when I kiss you?"

"You're so good," she answered brokenly. "So honest, so dependable . . . so kind."

"It sounds like a domestic servant's reference," he said wryly, and Jennie found she was actually able to laugh.

"That's better!" he rallied her. "This is the second time in two days you've wept in my arms. Is it that you're still worried about your father?"

She rested her head on his shoulder and the strength

of his arm about her was comforting. "It's not Father," she told him, because this was the moment when evasions between them must cease. "It's myself. I'm not good enough for you, John . . . No, don't interrupt!" She laid a hand lightly across his lips. "I think I've been too shallow in my thoughts about . . . us. I've taken our relationship too lightly. I don't know what I expected from it . . . that we might go on forever the way we were. Perhaps the truth is that I didn't think deeply about it at all. You were there, and I took our friendship for granted. And then when you spoke of marriage . . . I woke up with a bang."

"But darling, if that's how you feel we don't have to talk of marriage. Not yet . . . not until you're ready for it. I've been clumsy, selfish. . . ."

"No, no!" she interrupted him. "It's I who've been selfish, stupid, not realising what a wonderful person you are."

"Now hold on, darling!" he halted her in embarrassment. "I'm not in the least wonderful, nor specially unselfish."

"You *are,* John." And suddenly she was looking up into his face with such an air of revelation that he could only kiss her again.

"I mean I'd be proud to marry you," she heard herself declare. It was true, she assured herself. John was strong, and above all sincere. He would never lie to her, trick her. And he loved her. At this moment he was a refuge to run to, a shelter from the nightmare blackness which threatened to engulf her, a nightmare she couldn't wholly realise yet. But she knew that it waited for her . . . would have to be dealt with, looked at, accepted in all its ugliness. Belonging to John would help her in this. John would help her in everything from now on as long as she lived. And in return she would learn to forget herself, serve him . . . love him as devotedly as he now loved her.

The rest of the evening had a dreamlike quality. They went back to the ballroom and danced for a while, and Jennie's glance went sharply across the floor to the white and gold foyer with its adjacent lounges and bars it was not that she was dreading a glimpse of Glyn Harney, she assured herself. She didn't care now if she never saw him again. He had ceased to exist for her and there was a grim satisfaction in deciding that he was probably somewhere around with his two brash young colleagues, drinking himself silly while he boasted about his successful capture of the elusive Adrian Romaine. If her anger stirred at the thought, it was a stimulating anger, carrying her through what was left of the evening with a convincing show of cheerfulness.

But alone in her own room at last, the nightmare with its spectres drew close, and she lay in her bed writhing with humiliation, and a bitter sense of loss. It was not only Glyn Harney who had gone, but her faith in herself. All she had thought about him had been a myth. She had made it all up, let her imagination run away with her, fancying she had met in this stranger the twin soul who would bring her fulfilment. "My heart answers your heart," she had told him, and burying her face in her pillows felt her cheeks hot with shame. How could she have been so credulous, so blind! Clinging to the thought of him even after he had said to her, "I can't mean anything to you, Jennie. You must put me out of your mind."

After he had got all he wanted from her! His entrée into the Romaine household. Planning and scheming for it, pretending not to know who she was that first morning on the quayside, then probing with seeming delicacy and subtlety until she revealed herself as Romaine's daughter. Oh, it was all so clever, so mean . . . so cruel!

For hours she lay staring into the darkness, letting the pain sweep over her. It's like a physical illness, she thought. And like an illness it would spend itself . . . and she would recover. After tonight she would turn her back on Glyn Harney and all that concerned him. She would not waste one more tremor of emotion on him.

Somehow she slept at last, and woke in the morning feeling cold and strong and resolute. It was Steamer

Day, she remembered; Sir Mark would be leaving the island at three o'clock. During the morning he and John spent some time with the invalid. Then they all had lunch together on the terrace, Adrian joining them, rejoicing that he had been released from his sickroom imprisonment and could sit up at the luncheon table. "Like a Christian", as he said. Meals served on a solitary tray never tasted quite right. Dympna in one of her more angelic moods leaned against his knee and shared the peach he peeled for dessert. Jennie was reassured as she watched him. The threat of that heart attack really seemed to have retreated, and he was almost his old self again, although there were emphatic warnings from Sir Mark before he left as to the care that was still needed.

John and Jennie went down to the quay to see the great man off. His goodbye embrace for Jennie was affectionately paternal.

"Why don't you come back to London with John at the end of the month?" he suggested. "We should be delighted to have you pay us a visit and you could be looking the Harley Street flat over, deciding with John what decorations you would like and so on. Several of the rooms need doing over. . . ."

John was all enthusiasm for the idea. "If we're really going to get married in the autumn we ought to get cracking with the preliminary arrangements."

"Of course you're going to be married in the autumn," Sir Mark put in, faintly puzzled. "It's all settled, isn't it?"

"Yes, it's absolutely settled," Jennie told him, with a warm glance in John's direction. And thanking her future father-in-law for his invitation, she agreed that she would love to accept it, providing her father was well enough to be left.

"I don't think you need to worry on that score," Sir Mark assured her. "Adrian has made marked progress during the last few days, and he will have Sister Therese to look after him and see that he keeps to his resting routine and so on."

"I wouldn't want to be away from him too long,"

Jennie temporised. "Not more than a fortnight, per-haps."

"But that's no time at all," John objected. "There'll be so much to see to . . . choosing the decorations for the flat and so on."

It wasn't concern for the decorating of the flat which brought the hot possessive gleam to his eyes. Once he got her in London he wouldn't easily let her go.

"Just see how it works out," Sir Mark advised. "Don't make any rigid time limits. We shall be so happy to have you with us, Jennie dear. I know Dorothy will be delighted to hear that you're coming."

A warning outburst from the ship's siren ended the conversation and Sir Mark hurried aboard.

Driving back to the villa Jennie thought of the visit to which she had committed herself. Somehow it made her feel much more definitely engaged to John, who, sitting by her side, made enthusiastic plans about all they would do when they got home.

Jennie heard the last word with a small constriction of her heart. 'Home'. But of course it was the right word. John's home would be hers too—no matter how difficult it was to visualise it at the moment. Two spacious floors over the professional ground floor where Sir Mark had his consulting rooms and surgery. The Davenhams had never lived in it, letting it to a series of tenants. Their residence was an imposing house in a quiet, exclusive crescent, overlooking Regent's Park. And Lady Davenham—Sir Mark's wife Dorothy—efficient as she was elegant, saw that it was run with clockwork precision. Jennie, who had never seen her with a hair out of place, was rather in awe of her. A perfectionist in all that she did—nothing ever seemed to ruffle her or throw her off course. She was a mother-in-law it might be difficult to live up to. But she would tackle that hurdle when she came to it, Jennie decided sensibly.

After that life settled down to its pleasant summer holiday routine. Swimming and lazing in the morning sunshine on one or other of the delectable beaches with which the island abounded. Most of them undiscovered so far by the Slavonia's clientele. After lunch on the terrace and a brief nap in one of the seductive lounge chairs under the vine leaves Jennie and John would get into the car and explore the hinterland in a leisurely fashion, often leaving the car to climb one of the rugged stony hills, wandering off the beaten track to find lonely little villages where life went its sleepy way, aeons removed from the bustle of the twentieth century. Frequently they stayed out until the late summer darkness fell, eating a simple evening meal at some wayside inn, drinking the mild sweet red wine. John invariably drove on the way home, Jennie, sleepy with food and wine and sunshine, leaning comfortably with her head on his shoulder. When they stopped by the way for kisses and caresses she found herself responding with a growing warmth. It was all as it should be, she told herself. She was happy, quietly and undeviatingly happy, with the kind of happiness which lasts; no exaggerated heights, or depths, no emotional storms. Just John being his own dear kind placid self day after golden day.

It was nothing to her, she told herself, that Glyn Harney often spent an hour or more in the studio with her father, planning the prospective television talks. There had to be a good deal of rehearsal before it came to an actual recording of the conversations. Several times the cameramen were included in these sessions. Twice Adrian invited the three men up to the villa for coffee and drinks. But each time Jennie was carefully absent, and on the rare occasions when she found herself briefly face to face with Glyn she greeted him distantly, a state of affairs he seemed to take for granted. She was busy with her fiancé and could not be expected to have any time for anyone else. Nor would this disturb him. He had got what he wanted from her during his first few days on the island, she reminded herself bitterly. How she chose to behave subsequently would be of little interest to him.

That, at all events, was how she interpreted his aloof manner, telling herself she couldn't have cared less. Since that evening at the Slavonia when she had found out what he really was like he had ceased to exist for her. What pain she had suffered had been for her own lost foolish dream, and her humiliation. And now, she could assure herself, it was not only that Glyn Harney had ceased to exist for her . . . he had *never* existed. The man she had envisaged had been a figment of her imagination. So that she could look now at the Glyn Harney who occasionally appeared as if he were the blankest of blank strangers. Thus her triumph over her brief infatuation was complete. Had it been achieved a little too easily? A question she did not ask herself. In self-examination there are limits it may be wise to observe. So she took a day at a time and was thankful for their quiet happiness and unruffled calm. John loved her. John was trustworthy. With John she was safe.

Then, all too soon, the weeks of his holiday on Zelen were drawing to a close. In two days' time he and Jennie would be boarding the familiar steamer on the first stage of their journey to London—a fact, which creeping up on her, seemed to catch her unawares.

As usual, she thought, I've been drifting along, enjoying the passing moment, not looking ahead. Facing up to realities, she decided wryly, was not her strong point. It was not going to be easy to leave her father. But she would come back to him as soon as she could. Flat or no flat, marriage plans or no marriage plans, she would make her stay in London as short as possible. There was little enough time left to spend with her father. After October it was John who would have the first claim on her days, her nights, her love . . . her duty.

When she pointed out something of this to Adrian he remarked that marriage would not take her all that far away from him, at least not in a geographical sense.

She was sitting on his bed, having come to his room for a goodnight chat.

"We shall be living only a couple of miles apart," he reminded her practically. "You will be able to come along to Riverside Walk every day if you still want to be bothered with your old father."

A remark which sent her into his arms—as no doubt

he had guessed it would. "Nothing can ever really divide us, my Jennie," he told her, ruffling her hair. "And this little trip to London with John is neither here nor there. You'll soon be back here again, and October is a long time off. There are still many weeks for us to spend together in the old way. Such a happy way. I've been very fortunate in my youngest daughter, Jennie dear! I don't know what I should have done without you in my declining years, filling the empty places in my somewhat battered heart."

She thought of her brilliantly clever intellectual mother, so often away from home, or if at home, absorbed in her own affairs.

She stood up, smoothing the tumbled bedcovers. In a moment or two Sister Therese would be arriving with the patient's nightcap, a glass of hot milk.

"Darling Papa," she whispered, "I don't know how I'm going to get along without you."

"You won't have to get along without me," he reiterated cheerfully. "I'll be right there on your doorstep, making a nuisance of myself."

"But it won't be the same."

"No," he agreed, "it won't be quite the same ... for you it will be better. That's what comforts me; the thought of you being safe with John."

"Safe?" she questioned. But he did not answer the question.

"Things change," he said. "Relationships alter. Nothing lasts for ever in this transient world. That's something we have to learn to accept."

What was he trying to say to her? There was a wistfulness in his tone that smote Jennie's heart. She looked down at the sharpened outlines of his face. Illness had altered him, given him a fragile transparent air, and noticing it now for the first time she felt the cold breath of fear. Pushing it away from her, she cried out, "Nothing is going to change between us, Papa, I will not let things change. Never, never."

"Sweet child, you're very young," he sighed. "All I ask is that you may know great happiness with your

John. You *are* happy with him, aren't you?" he ended a little anxiously.

There had been moments recently when he had noticed shadows in her eyes. Shadows which ought not to be there—during these early days of her engagement, days which surely should be among the happiest in her life.

"Of course I'm happy with John . . . my darling John. I adore him!" Jennie cried out, and her smile was so radiant, her tone so convincing that her father was reassured.

CHAPTER TEN

IT was at breakfast time the following morning when Claire said, "Let's have a party at the Slavonia for Jennie and John's last evening. Give them a royal send-off. We've never celebrated their engagement properly and this would be an opportunity."

Jennie said a little doubtfully, "I've packed all my evening gear."

"Then unpack it again," Claire ordered light-heartedly.

"Do you think Papa would be well enough to come with us?" Jennie asked. Unless he was, there would be no party, she had already decided. She wasn't going to waste her last evening on Zelen dancing at the Slavonia while he stayed at home alone.

"What does Doctor John say?" Claire asked, smiling at him confidently across the table as though she was sure his answer would be favourable.

He hedged a bit. "Personally I'm all in favour. If he took things easily the change of scene and the jollification and so on would do him a lot of good. I'll have to see how he feels about it . . . and Dr Sinjek must be consulted. I'll have a word with him on the blower after I've seen your father."

Adrian, of course, thought the party a splendid idea. Dr Sinjek was inclined to be doubtful, but after a little argument on John's part was persuaded that Mr Romaine might be permitted a couple of hours at the Slavonia. He must, however, be back home and in bed by half past ten. Sister Therese could collect him by taxi—so that the party need not be broken up.

So in a very short time it was all arranged, Claire having contacted the hotel and ordered a specially chosen meal suitable for the celebration of an engagement.

They would like a secluded table, she had added, with plenty of flowers for decoration.

Adrian, after a little preliminary grumbling at the conditions imposed by Dr Sinjek, was so elated at the prospect of the party that Jennie began to be more enthusiastic about it herself. But she wished Claire hadn't been so specific with the hotel management about the reason for it—an engagement celebration. The maître d'hôtel would be delighted. One never knew to what lengths a Continental hotelier would go to when presented with so romantic an assignment. She and John would be the centre of attention, seated side by side at the head of the table—presented no doubt with special floral favours. She must look her best, wear her most glamorous dress. She chose a slim, tight-fitting white silk, flared exaggeratedly at the hem with a frill of flounces which foamed round her ankles. The bodice was embroidered with apricot-coloured flowers and there was a filmy scarf of the same colour to match. It was a dress she had bought for an evening opening of one of her father's exhibitions in Paris and she had only worn it once. Now, as she surveyed it in the mirror, it seemed to her very bridal. But why not? Tonight was a bridal occasion. Strange how the thought of her marriage to John could still strike her at odd moments as completely unreal. It was because of her habit of living in the present moment, she told herself. Anything in the future could so easily seem unreal.

John, waiting for her in the hall, gasped as she came down the stairs, a vision of white and gold. He was taking her to the hotel in the two-seater, the rest of the family having gone in the larger car. "You look too beautiful to be touched!" he told her.

"But I'm not," she laughed, and throwing her arms round his neck kissed him wholeheartedly.

The car's canvas roof cover was folded back, but fortunately it was a warm windless evening. It was on the way down the hairpin track to the town that John broke it to Jennie that Adrian, who had had Glyn Harney in the studio during that afternoon had in a burst of ill-timed hospitality invited him to join them at the Slavonia. It was his gregarious, generous way and it evidently hadn't occurred to him that the party was a strictly family affair.

"It isn't as if we're short of a man," Claire grumbled indignantly to her sister when they were putting a final touch to hair and make-up in one of the Slavonia's luxurious cloakrooms.

Jennie, applying lipstick with an amazingly steady hand, said in a cold voice, "I certainly could have done without the slick Mr Harney at my engagement party." Beneath the coldness rage simmered. If only she had known what Papa was going to do . . . if only she could have stopped him! But it was too late now. The only thing left to her was to ignore Glyn, refuse to let him spoil her evening.

As she and Claire entered the lounge the three men waiting stood to greet them. "Here comes the bride!" Adrian exclaimed jocularly. Jennie began to wish she had put on a less obvious dress.

"Miss Jennie, my felicitations!" Glyn Harney held out a hand, which she had to take, and it seemed to her that it was in a half mocking way he bowed over it. She lifted her eyes to meet his glance. But there was nothing of mockery in the dark blue eyes. It was as if at that moment, everything she had once imagined he felt about her flashed for an instant in their depths. Hurriedly she clamped down on the response the intense look evoked. She wasn't going to be fooled, even in the slightest degree by the mannerisims or glances of this despicable man. She was far too taken up with John, she told herself, even to be bothered despising Glyn Harney. He wasn't worth the least tremor of emotion.

They did not linger over aperitifs, remembering poor Adrian's medical time limit, and by eight sharp they went into the great dining room to find their special table, large and round, set in a deep window with a superb view of woodland bays and hills. Claire exclaimed at the trouble the management had taken over the decorations. "They certainly let themselves go," she murmured a trifle doubtfully.

"I knew you ought not to have said anything about an engagement," Jennie whispered to her reproachfully. The flowers were all white, tied with silver ribbons, the centrepiece a cluster of white and silver, crowned with an archway of little silver bells. There were favours of white and silver at every set place, and a trail of smilax in front of the young couple's seats enclosed the words in English, 'Felicitations to bride and groom'.

"A bit previous, aren't they?" Jacques remarked, while Jennie, all her carefully built up detachment collapsing, blushed crimson. John, enjoying the situation to the full, laughingly embraced her and dropped a light kiss on her brow.

After that the party went with a swing. If Jennie wasn't quite caught up in the prevailing mood nobody noticed it. The food was delicious, the champagne perfectly chilled and had just the right touch of dryness. A toast was drunk to the happiness of Jennie and John, Adrian insisting upon making a ceremonious little speech. Tucked away in their window embrasure and with the dining room barely half full, since most people dined late, the setting was sufficiently private to avoid the embarrassment of attracting attention. And the Slavonia clientele was not composed of visitors who would be likely to recognise Adrian. Though Glyn Harney, Jennie noticed, the television personality, rated an inquisitive glance or two. Seated opposite to him at the big round table it was impossible to be altogether unaware of him, Jennie was finding. For all her brave resolves to ignore him he was spoiling the party for her ... and she hated him.

Then all too soon it was ten o'clock and Adrian, like an elderly male Cinderella, was whisked away by the devoted Sister Therese, to be taken home in one of the local taxi-cabs. Claire, cleverly negotiating this interruption which might well have ruined the evening's atmosphere, moved her diminished forces out on to one of the balconies that overlooked the illuminated garden. Fairy lamps in the trees and a floodlit swimming pool: but beyond it all lay the magic vista of the night-dark sea and glimmering white beach. The width of the great dining room lay between them and the ballroom so that the dance music was pleasantly muted. And presently John and Jennie went off to dance. Claire and Glyn soon followed. Jennie tried not to watch them, concentrating on the pleasure of John's skilled partnering. He was a nimble and inventive dancer with a wonderful sense of rhythm and Jennie was fully occupied going along with him. But at the back of her mind she was wondering what she would do if Glyn should ask her to dance with him. Something like panic stirred in her heart. She turned from it fiercely, holding on to her determination that whatever happened she would remain emotionally uninvolved.

Soon after they returned to coffee and liqueurs on the balcony the moment she had dreaded was upon her. Glyn, having brought Claire back from the dance floor, turned to Jennie with a casual, "Would you care to have this one with me, Miss Romaine?"

"No, I should hate to!" she longed to cry out. But it would be too dramatic. Glyn wasn't worth a scene. So she went with him wordlessly, forcing herself to take his offered arm.

The orchestra was playing a dreamy waltz tune. They could sway to its rhythm in the contemporary fashion, or treat it in the orthodox manner, slowly circling the floor. And that apparently was what Glyn decided upon. His arm about her waist was light, his palm on which the tips of her fingers rested cool and firm. They did not speak and Jennie didn't dare to look up at him, horrified to find herself completely thrown off balance by his nearness, his touch. Where now was her beautiful detachment? With every nerve in her body she was aware of him. This was the first time she had danced with him, and in a way it conveyed more intimacy than his few tentative kisses had done. It was a contact that lasted. It went on and on, making her feel dizzy, bemusing her senses. It was almost a relief when he spoke, though the last thing she wanted was any kind of conversation with him.

He said, "I know you've been very much occupied since your fiancé arrived, Jennie, but I can't help having noticed your rather odd manner towards myself. Not once in the last couple of weeks have you addressed one word to me, even when you found me with your father in the studio. I hope I'm not being unduly touchy, but I wondered if anything was wrong, if I'd in some unthinking way offended you?"

Unthinking! The nerve of the man! A great flame of anger leaped up within her, shaking her, robbing her of clear thought. And he had sounded so desolate as he spoke ... reproachful almost. If only she could control the storm of resentment that possessed her, dismiss his question with a coolly delivered snub. Was anything wrong indeed!

"Wrong!" she burst out. "Nothing's wrong ... only that I've discovered that you're capable of the sort of crooked scheming, dishonourable behaviour that makes me sick!" She leaned back in his dance-floor embrace to look up at him, her eyes blazing. "Why did you pretend you hadn't recognised me as Adrian Romaine's daughter that day I first met you ... coming off the steamer?"

"So that's it!" She heard him draw in a harsh breath.

"Yes, that's it," she confirmed grimly. "I was waiting in the foyer of the Slavonia for my fiancé the evening after your cameramen arrived on the island. They happened to be sitting in a couple of armchairs behind my rather concealing settee and I heard them recounting your triumph. How you had fooled the Romaine girl along, until you got her to invite you up to the Villa and introduce you to her father as some kind of learned Balkan historian. Trapping him into receiving you, hiding your real purpose as a prowling TV newsman on the hunt for an all-time scoop. And you got it! My father in the end offering to collaborate with you over a series of talks on his paintings. You couldn't be done boasting about it, it seems. . . ."

She felt his fingers fold convulsively over her own.

There were white lines about his mouth and his jaw tensed. "That isn't quite how it was, Jennie. I wasn't entirely sure of your identity that morning on the quayside. I'd seen a press photograph of you with your father at one of his openings. Then on that memorable evening at Urbino you told me your name. . . ."

"And from then on it was plain sailing," Jennie said bitterly.

"On the contrary; I felt the only thing I could do was to let the whole Romaine project drop." There was a pause before he added softly, "Perhaps because I'd become far too personally involved."

Once more she looked up at him and seeing the pain in his eyes her anger suddenly deserted her and a great surge of sorrow took its place. "I can't mean anything to you. You must forget me," he had told her that night he had waited for her in the dusk at the villa gate . . . willing her to come out to him. And, mysteriously impelled, she had obeyed.

"You tried to warn me," she conceded. Weakly she leaned against him. His arm tightened about her and for a moment they did not speak. A feeling of well-being enfolded her, of quietness and utter peace.

"If only you'd been honest with me," she said in a low, trembling voice.

"Perhaps I might have been, but you invited me to the Villa, said your father wanted to meet me. The temptation to keep silent at that point was far too great for me."

"So you boasted to your camera crew that you'd 'made' the unsuspecting Romaine girl and were to be admitted into the sacred precincts of the great man's studio." Anger was returning, reviving her. Anger that was safe and must be held on to, encouraged. Whatever emerged she must go on hating and despising this man. She drew in a quick breath that to her horror sounded like a sob. And she was still close in Glyn's arms, leaning against him, needing his strength, her heart in spite of her responding to his nearness. And somewhere, deeper than reason, lay the feeling that he was incapable of the perfidy with which she had accused him. And that he loved her.

She closed her eyes and heard him say, "Oh, Jennie, dear Jennie! How can I make you believe that I never spoke of you to my camera boys in the way you imply? I gave them only the barest details of my meeting with you and of my subsequent invitation to meet your father. How could I have cheapened our association, feeling about it the way I do?" The last words were barely audible. But she heard them. And here under the garish lights of the ballroom the truth that was in his heart called to the truth that was in hers. The strange illogical truth—which had nothing to do with the treason of his silences, his withholding of his identity until his conquest of Adrian Romaine had been secure. A television network spy. For that was the cold, realistic summing up of his behaviour and she must never lose sight of it. The pain that swept over her made her feel physically sick. But she clung to it. It was the pain that was the truth—the pain of her utter disillusion. Everything else was passing madness.

"Take me back to the others," she pleaded. "I can't dance with you any more."

Her pallor alarmed him. With an arm lightly about her shoulders he guided her through the ranks of dancers, and across the glittering dining room to the balcony where Claire and Jacques and John awaited them.

"Jennie isn't feeling very well," Jennie heard Glyn say. And it was John's arm about her then, John rescuing her from her own nightmare weakness, her traitorous heart.

"It's all right." She managed a shaky laugh. "It was just the heat of the ballroom, I think, and going round and round in that old-fashioned waltz step...." She hardly knew what she was saying, but it didn't matter. Something inside her was dying. And the sooner it died the better. Let it die! She was glad of the muted light on the balcony as she sank into a deeply cushioned wicker lounge chair.

"I must admit I felt a bit dizzy myself just now when

I was waltzing with John," Claire was saying. "It's so long since I've done any old-fashioned waltzing. But it's a marvellous floating sensation when you get into it."

So John and Claire had been dancing together . . . and she hadn't noticed them, Jennie mused. Though they must have passed close to herself and Glyn several times as they circled the ballroom floor. Had there been anything conspicuous in the rather intense way they were talking to one another? Not that it mattered. Nothing mattered only that she must get through what was left of this nightmare evening as well as she could.

Leaning over her, full of solicitude, John was asking if there was anything he could get for her. "Some hot coffee," he offered. "Or an aspirin. They're sure to have aspirins at the reception desk."

Dear kind, practical John, who could cure a troubled heart with coffee and aspirins! Glyn had faded into the shadows behind Claire's chair, and everyone seemed slightly at a loss. The party was falling to pieces . . . and it was all her fault. She sat up resolutely and told John she didn't want any coffee or aspirins.

"I'm feeling perfectly all right," she asserted vigorously. "It was just a momentary vertigo, and coming out here into the fresh air has completely banished it."

She swung herself out of the long chair. "Let's go and watch the cabaret show," she suggested. Sounds from the ballroom indicated that it had just started.

"A jolly good idea," Jacques agreed with an air of relief. Too bad if the party broke up with a fainting bride-to-be! And from what he had heard it was quite a good floor show they put on at the Slavonia, even if it hadn't quite the artistic appeal of the *kolo* being danced in a village street.

CHAPTER ELEVEN

LONDON towards the end of August looked pretty tired and dusty. In all the main streets and most of the lesser thoroughfares the build-up of traffic was becoming intolerable. The noise was stupefying and never-ending, the atmosphere a suffocating mixture of exhaust fumes and humanity. Jennie, in her journeying back and forth between Regent's Park and Harley Street, thought wistfully of the thyme-scented peace of Zelen.

Already, in spite of that optimistically visualised fortnight, her time in London had stretched to almost a month. And there was still much to be done. The painters and decorators hadn't quite finished with the rooms of the flat and after they had gone there would be the carpeting and curtaining to supervise, to say nothing of the installing of the furniture and fitting up of the small, beautifully modern kitchen. Gazing about her, Jennie would try to imagine how it would all be when she and John lived in these unfamiliar rooms. Sometimes she made little sketches, drawing up plans for the way she wanted to arrange the furniture. Some of it was valuable family stuff donated by the Davenhams, but much of it was being chosen by herself and Lady Davenham in their numerous visits to the more exclusive London emporiums.

It was all costing a great deal of money, but it never entered Jennie's head to worry about that. Her father had made a considerable fortune from the sale of his paintings, and money flowed in and out of the Romaine household with equal ease. The Davenhams, too, were well-heeled, and John was their only child. Both families were determined to give the young couple a good start in their married life. It was very kind of them . . . and everything was wonderful. Jennie wished she could feel a little more enthusiastic about it all, but she was still haunted by that indefinable sense of unreality. With her reprehensible tendency to drift from day to day she would realise every now and then that she did not clearly envisage the future which was bringing her married state so near. In a few weeks' time she would be Mrs John Davenham.

It might have been better if she could have seen more of John, but it was only at week-ends and not always then that he was free. Like most young newly qualified doctors he worked long hours at his hospital, and when he was not on call there he had to put in hours of study for his consultancy examination, a hurdle he must face before he would be able to become his father's partner to any useful extent.

However, on the rare occasions when he could spare the time they went off in his mile-devouring sports car to the country. And these expeditions, Jennie told herself, were all that they should be, the weather kindly, the landscape, after they had left the suburbs, all harvest fields and rolling downs. Usually they ended up by the sea, the cool grey English Channel, so different from the jade green waters of the Adriatic. If John in the seclusion of some woodland layby became demonstrative she did her best to respond. But usually he seemed content just to be with her, talking, or not talking in the easy fashion of their long association. Sometimes, during one of their silences, she would catch him studying her in an oddly questioning way. But the questions, if there were any, were never asked, and Jennie did not probe. They were happy together in a quiet way, content in one another's company. Best leave it like that. It would all be so different when they were married, she told herself. Engagements were notoriously a difficult time; a sort of limbo when you were neither one thing or the other, neither wholly attached, nor unattached.

Occasionally when there was an hour or two to spare from the flat decorating and shopping Jennie would slip away to the big family house on Riverside Walk, where Mrs Tracey, their elderly housekeeper, welcomed her with open arms. Jennie would drink tea with her in the pleasant little sitting room off the basement kitchen and then wander about the large, not very well kept rooms of the ground floor and above. It was all so different from the immaculate order at Regency Terrace, touched with a Bohemian disorder that Jennie recognised as 'home.' "*Things*," Adrian Romaine had often declared, "shall never dominate me." If the furniture was shabby, the carpets worn, it did not matter. Beauty was not to be found in immaculately polished and dusted rooms. Rooms were for living in, and living was an unidy affair. So was the creation of beauty. Up on the top floor where the wide studio stretched over two large attics with the intervening wall removed, Jennie would linger, looking at her father's work and longing for the moment when she could get back to him.

He was getting on well, Claire wrote, improving daily. "Glyn Harney," she had said in her last letter, "seems to give him just the stimulus he needs. They still spend hours over that everlasting script, but it's nearly finished, I gather, and in a few days' time Glyn Harney will be departing, taking his spoils back to his triumphant TV network in London."

So Glyn would soon be sharing this vast city with herself, Jennie mused. But the chances of their running into one another were so remote as to be non-existent—a conclusion she reviewed with satisfaction. That was the only time his name had been mentioned in any of Claire's letters, and Jennie congratulated herself that she had succeeded in putting him completely out of her mind. Even the thought that he would shortly be breathing the same petrol-laden air as herself failed to stir her in the smallest degree.

What did excite her was that her mother was shortly returning from America and the long lecture tour, full of delight about the approaching wedding. If she had not come back earlier when Adrian was taken ill it was because he had refused to allow her to be told of what he called his 'mild seizure'. The American tour was important to her, an acknowledgement of her years of hard work as a novelist and speaker on a wide variety of subjects. Her interests were largely concerned with world problems, social and environmental, and she took them seriously. If she was inclined to give herself more to 'causes' than to her family it worked out all right. Adrian was absorbed in his career as she was in hers and on this basis they seemed to have formed a good relationship. And Jennie with a father who adored her did not feel deprived by her mother's public life. That her mother loved her, she had never doubted, and she admired her for her achievements. The times they *did* spend together were always stimulating, full of happenings. They entertained a good deal when she was at home, and Jennie met all sorts of interesting people. Life she thought now had been very good in the riverside house. But there was no reason why she should not still share in it after she married. It would always be her second home, she comforted herself, it wasn't all that far from the Harley Street flat.

Then early in September another letter came from Claire, reminding Jennie that she had been away far too long.

"Now that Glyn Harney has gone," she wrote, "Papa is feeling rather deserted, and misses you. Besides, I ought to be getting back to Paris with Dympna and Nannie. Jacques had to return there a couple of weeks ago and he's no good on his own—misses his family. Mama will be here to help you to shut up the villa for the winter. Dr Sinjek thinks Papa ought to return to England a little earlier this year than he usually does. He—Dr Sinjek—says Papa has had enough of our sultry autumn heat and that a change to a brisker climate would help him. It isn't that he's any worse, but he did have a slight turn the other day. It was his own fault. Sister Therese, as you know, has long since departed, and without her eagle eye on him he started painting again and made himself very tired.

"Anyway, do try to get back here within the next few days and you'll see for yourself how things are."

Jennie's first reaction to this letter was an immense sense of release. To be back in Zelen again 'in a few days' time'—the responsibility of flats and weddings left behind. And her father was missing her. She smothered the feeling of alarm at the news of the slight 'turn'. But it would convince Lady Davenham—and John—that for the moment there were more important matters in her life than the colour of curtains.

When she told John of her summons to Zelen he gave her one of his inscrutable looks. "You want to go, don't you?" It sounded faintly accusing, but he had come home late after a long day at the hospital and wasn't perhaps at his most tactful.

"I have been away rather a long time," Jennie reminded him. "And now if Papa isn't quite so well, and is missing me.. . ."

"Of course, my love," John agreed. "I know you must go. I'm just being selfish."

"Why don't you come too?" Jennie suggested, and instantly John's nice open face, that could never quite hide his feelings, cleared.

"Maybe I could, at that! Snatch a long week-end off. I can't manage it right away, but I could work it in a little later. Catch that Friday steamer from Rijeka, and return by the Tuesday boat. . . ."

"Zelen in September," Jennie sighed blissfully. "Think of it! The water still warm and the sun as hot as ever. All the ripe fruit, the grape harvest, the wine making, the figs. . . ." She smacked her lips. "Let's ring up the travel agent and make my flight reservation right away!"

The very next evening Lady Davenham, who negotiated the worst tangles of London traffic with her usual unruffled efficiency, drove her to Heathrow. There was real affection in her farewell embrace. She was very lucky to have such a thoroughly nice prospective mother-in-law, Jennie reflected as she took her seat in the big jet, already throbbing with the power which presently would sweep it up off the runway.

Soon they were over France, heading southwards through the darkness to arrive at Rijeka at the ungodly hour of two a.m. There was time for a brief rest at a portside hotel before Jennie dragged herself sleepily to the harbour to catch the steamer for Modice. She slept solidly all the way, waking to find the early morning light spilling down over the familiar market stalls on the quayside.

Involuntarily her glance went towards the *kafana* where Glyn had taken her that memorable morning she had had the encounter with the ship's crane. For an instant the whole scene before her was vivid with the memory. Then she spotted Claire in the knot of people waiting by the gangway, and the urgency in her sister's pale uplifted face effectively banished Glyn Harney and all concerning him from her thoughts. Something was seriously wrong!

"What is it?" she asked Claire breathlessly, even before they had time to exchange a kiss of greeting. "Is it Papa. . . ?"

Claire nodded. "Thank goodness you've come! He's been asking for you. He had another of his turns last evening—quite a bad one this time. Sister Therese is once more in office and Dr Sinjek has been fussing back and forth all night.

"But don't look so scared, darling!" she added rather unconvincingly. "You know how quickly Papa recovers. He seemed quite a lot better when I looked in on him just before I came to meet you. In fact he was demanding his breakfast just as if nothing had happened. But I won't hurry off to Paris and leave you as I'd planned," she added. "I'll stay for a few days to see how he gets on."

CHAPTER TWELVE

JENNIE thought the brief drive up the hill would never end. She couldn't be quick enough leaping out of the car and running up the stairs to see for herself how her father really was.

He greeted her with delight, and the sight of him propped up on his pillows, a breakfast tray before him—just as Claire had promised—did much to reassure her. Perhaps the worst was over. With heart trouble at his age the odd attack was probably inevitable. And Zelen, this September morning, was torrid with the sultry heat of a southern late summer. He would be all right when they got him back to the fresher air of England.

In spite of the breakfast tray they managed to exchange a comprehensive hug. There wasn't indeed very much on the tray; merely a cup of some milky-looking liquid. "Baby food," he said, indicating it with disgust. "Sinjek is such a fusspot. There's really very little wrong with me. The whole thing is a plot. Sinjek has a wild passion for our quiet little Sister Therese and this is a ruse to get her back into his orbit once more."

Jennie laughed dutifully, though it wasn't a very good joke, and regarding her father more observantly she was aware of the drawn look on his face, the deep shadows about his hollow eyes.

"You shouldn't have tried painting," she reproached him.

"I had to," he declared impenitently. "You know how I feel about the value of pictures nowadays, how they become nothing more than money-making symbols when they fall into the hands of the agents and art dealers. I thought I might be able to keep my cathedral painting out of all that racket by not signing it. So instead, now that it's finished I decided to paint a small self-portrait in the bottom right-hand corner. It has, though I say it myself, turned out to be a very successful little ruse. Harney would approve, I'm sure."

"He wouldn't approve of your having made yourself ill again," Jennie said severely.

Adrian made a grimace. "You haven't come home to scold me, darling. It's so wonderful to see you again. Go and fetch your own breakfast tray and have your coffee and rolls here with me and tell me all about London."

Only too gladly Jennie complied, promising Sister Therese whom she met on her way from the kitchen that she wouldn't let her father talk too much or get over-excited.

"If you need me I shall be out on the terrace having breakfast with Madame Lemaître," she said.

But they wouldn't need her, Jennie decided hopefully. Adrian, apart from his fragile looks, seemed so very much his usual self. When she was settled with her tray at a small table by his bedside conversation flowed. She tried to explain all that was being done to the Harley Street flat, but somehow she couldn't make it sound very interesting. Her voice only came to life when she told of her visits to the Chelsea house and her cups of tea with comfortable Mrs Tracey. "Your studio is just as you left it," she assured him. "Everything is ready for you to come home to."

Inevitably he spoke of Glyn Harney, and of the recorded television talks. "I can't tell you how helpful and inspiring he was, drawing me out, guiding the conversation along just the right lines. He is so extraordinarily understanding and sensitive ... about me ... about Zelen and my feeling for the place. He made me talk of it in a way I didn't know I could. I suddenly found a sort of ... eloquence, like painting with words. No one but Harney could have bewitched me into it. It was odd feeling that it was all being taped for reproduction on a television screen, my words, my thoughts being preserved in this novel fashion. It made me feel a little less guilty over my laziness in never having attempted to write any kind of memoirs."

"And you didn't feel it was all a kind of publicity stunt?" Jennie asked.

"It wasn't publicity, but communication, Harney assured me."

Jennie felt a flicker of scorn. How cleverly Glyn had manipulated the old man!

"It will be my message to posterity," Adrian went on, with no sense of pompousness. "An attempt to convey something of the happiness I've felt in a long life of painting. And it will be a tribute to Zelen, my island. If I could help, even in the smallest way, to preserve the spirit of this beautiful place, then I feel my painting of the cathedral and the words I have spoken about it will not have been in vain. Tourists will flock here when the big hotels are built and the air-strip completed. If they can be made to glimpse in my cathedral painting something of the life that has gone on here through the ages, the courage which fought off invaders in the past, which even now fights poverty and the domination of an alien form of government, then my efforts and Harney's will be worth while. And all this couldn't happen if my painting and the talks concerning it were not going to be given that maximum presentation which is only made possible by the television medium."

He paused, breathless, and as he lay back on his pillows Jennie saw the beads of moisture on his brow. "Darling, you're talking too much!" She wiped the drops of moisture away. "And Sister Therese warned me that I mustn't let you do that."

He held her hand, his own oddly cold in spite of the heat of the day. "There's so much to say," he whispered, "and so little time in which to say it."

What did he mean? For a moment her heart faltered. Thank God Claire had sent for her, and that she had come quickly.

But it was a happy day which followed. Later Jennie was to treasure the memory of it, for there were not many days left.

The end came peacefully, Sister Therese waking Jennie and Claire in the early hours one morning a few days later to say that it was all over. Adrian Romaine had died quietly in his sleep.

Jennie was shattered. It would take weeks, perhaps months before she could begin to adjust to the blank left by her father's death. Though she loved her mother and they got on well together, she had always been primarily her father's daughter, the child of his old age, to whom he had given a depth of affection not called forth by any of his other children. There had been a unique bond between them. And now the bond was broken. She moved through the first days of sad confusion and darkness in a stunned state. There was comfort of a sort when Karla, her mother, flew in post-haste from America, and John from London. Jacques came from Paris, leaving Dympna with her nannie there. The villa was filled with the sad activity of preparation for the funeral. It was Adrian's wish that he should be buried here in this island he had loved.

When the funeral was over there remained the task of winding up Adrian's affairs on Zelen. The Villa was now to be given up, not merely closed for the winter. There would be no more long Zelen summers. Preparing the paintings for their move to the studio in London was a major undertaking. Karla and Jennie, with the help of a professional packer, worked hard. Claire had returned to Paris with Jacques, to see to her family responsibilities. But it was good for Jennie that there was so much to do. John, who had remained for a few days to help, could obviously not be expected to neglect his hospital duties indefinitely, so the brunt of the work fell on Karla Romaine and her daughter. With Marie gallantly supporting them in the background, seeing that meals were eaten regularly and that the house was kept in such comfort as could be managed.

But at last it was finished and the final farewells to the beloved island had been said. The three women made their final journey on the familiar white steamer and at Rijeka Marie took a plane for Paris while Karla and Jennie boarded the jet bound for Heathrow. They arrived there one misty September evening, to be met by a rather weary-looking John. Doing obligatory hospital service as well as intensive studying, he was beginning to flag. Some of his boyish charm had faded, the lines of his face were stronger, more starkly drawn, and his eyes as they rested on Jennie had a hungry, questioning look—very different from the confident way in which they had regarded her all through the long years of their easy youthful friendship. Young Doctor Davenham, meeting the inexorable realities of his chosen profession, was growing up fast.

There was no need now for Jennie to be a guest at the mansion in Regency Terrace; her home was with her mother in the riverside house. For the time being in their need for one another they were very close experiencing together the sad business of facing life without the Adrian they had both in their different ways loved so dearly. They spoke one morning soon after their return from Zelen of the looming wedding. It had been planned for October, but Adrian's death had inevitably disrupted the preparations to a certain degree.

"Do you think," Jennie ventured, "it might be a good idea to put it off now until the spring? I don't feel like a wedding at the moment," she added rather oddly, as if her marriage to John was some kind of casual entertainment. "I mean, it seems too much of a festivity at this sad time. I can't seem to give my mind to it . . . and all it entails."

And what of your heart? Karla might have asked. But all she said was, "It's your life, my dear, you must make your own decisions about this. Have a quiet little chat with John and see how he feels."

It wasn't until several days later that the chance for the quiet little chat occurred, days during which Jennie had gone dutifully to the flat in Harley Street helping to put the final touches to the beautiful fittings. It was all so perfectly equipped now, so eminently ready to receive her in her role as its mistress that it was increasingly impossible to do anything less than accept the role. Not, she told herself, that she wanted to. But it was as if all the elegant furnishings, the Chippendale table and chairs in the dining room, the rose-carpeted bedroom with its white and gold fourposter bed, were drawing her into their luxurious net.

I'm being ordered about by furniture, she thought whimsically. But that was what a great part of domestic life was all about. 'Things' dominating one's life—something Adrian had never submitted to.

Then it was one of John's rare free evenings and he took her out to dinner. They went to a small intimate restaurant in Soho, where every table was discreetly hidden in its own little alcove. The pink-shaded lights were muted, the whole atmosphere almost too overtly discreet. A rendezvous for lovers; the perfect setting for that quiet chat Jennie had promised herself. But now that she had the opportunity she didn't know how to get started. And John was little help, concentrating on ordering the meal, and enjoying it when it was served, so that talk was desultory. Even when they were lingering over their coffee and liqueurs he rambled on about this and that, telling her hospital anecdotes, which even as he related them he seemed to lose interest in. It was as if he knew what was coming and was doing his best to fob it off. But in the end it was he who precipitated matters by saying in a carefully casual tone when they were almost on the point of leaving the restaurant: "Do you realise, darling, that we haven't yet fixed the exact date of our wedding?"

Jennie gulped down a final mouthful of black coffee to bolster her morale, and said hurriedly, avoiding his glance: "I was going to talk to you about that." She picked up a silver filigree basket of bon-bons and studied them earnestly. "I was wondering, in fact, if it might be better to put it off for a while; until the spring, perhaps. It seems rather too soon after my father's death." Her voice faltered over the last sentence and when she forced herself to look at last at John there were diamond drops on her lashes.

He said sadly, "Adrian was everything to you, wasn't he, Jennie? It was to please him that you agreed to marry me. You don't really want to, you know. I've suspected it for some time."

"John!" she gasped, startled. "What *are* you saying!"

"Only what must now be said. You don't *have* to marry me, Jennie."

"But the flat," she blurted. "All the new furniture . . . the notice in *The Times* . . . the wedding presents which have been arriving ever since our engagement was announced."

Were these the only reasons against their wedding cancellation? his imploring glance seemed to be asking. There was naked pain in his grey eyes.

"Wedding presents and newspaper notices, flats and furniture. . . ." he echoed. "All these things are non-essentials."

"But we can't let everybody down," she cried, scarcely knowing what she was saying above the confusion of her thoughts. John's attitude was so unexpected, such a shock.

"We can't let ourselves down," he corrected her. "There's only one valid reason for marriage, sweet Jennie." His voice faltered. "And for one of us that reason is missing."

"You mean," she faltered, "you think I don't love you . . . in the marrying way?"

"That's exactly what I do mean. I've never 'turned you on', as the saying goes. But I've seen another man do it. Glyn Harney."

The name dropped like a stone into the sudden silence.

Then John went on, "That last night of my holiday on Zelen when we had dinner at the Slavonia. I watched you dance with him . . . saw a look on your face which has never once been there for me."

"No, John, no!" Jennie cried, shaken and white, her eyes all black centres. "Glyn Harney is horrible, deceitful . . . everything I despise. . . ."

"Yet he could make you respond to him in a way I never can."

The slow colour flooded Jennie's cheeks. "What makes you so sure?"

John shrugged. "It was a pretty revealing dance you and he had together that evening, quite lost to your surroundings. You might have been alone in the middle of the wilderness for all any of the other dancers mattered to you ... including Claire and myself. And whatever you were talking about seemed to be having a pretty shattering effect on both of you."

"It was because," Jennie explained hastily, "I'd accused him of cheating his way into my father's friendship, coming to our house under false pretences. And, naturally enough, I suppose, he was defending himself hotly. Quite unconvincingly, I may add."

('How can I make you believe that I didn't speak to my camera boys about you in the way that you imply? Do you really believe I could have so cheapened our association . . . feeling about it the way I do?')

A conversation she must not remember, yet one she knew in her deepest heart she would never forget.

"Whether he convinced you of his integrity, or not, you were in love with Harney," John said bitterly.

"*Were*," Jennie repeated. "In the past tense."

John shook his head. "Whatever it may have been, past or present, it was something you've never had for me. You have a tell-tale face, my poor Jennie; hopelessly honest. Not only this evening but many times what you have imagined to be your secret thoughts cried out to me. The prospect of your marriage has never been quite real to you. But you were too kind to tell me so." He sighed and shrugged. "The time has come for us to face the fact that our engagement hasn't been exactly a success. Nor does it promise much in the way of lasting happiness."

"So you're turning me down," Jennie said, and involuntarily a great wave of relief swept over her, like a gust of fresh air. Because they were at last being totally honest with one another.

John took a bon-bon from the silver dish and started at it fixedly. "I think we're turning one another down.

I'm beginning to realise that I ought not to have even considered marriage until I'd got my consultancy, and even then, starting work as Father's partner would have kept me almost wholly occupied with surgery hours and visiting. I just wouldn't have had the time to be a good husband. I wouldn't have made you happy, I'm afraid. So there it is! It wouldn't have worked out, so we'd better forget about it."

If I'd loved you it would have worked out, Jennie thought guiltily. But aloud she said, "Oh, John, it's so awful. What shall we do about the flat?" Fourposter beds and Chippendale chairs rushed into her mind, reproaching her. And she couldn't bear to look at John, poor hurt John, eating his bon-bon with a casual air which didn't deceive her.

"I'll live in the flat," he said. "I shall enjoy having a pad of my own, instead of being for ever with my parents, much as I love them." He managed a smile. "After all, I'm a big boy now." He caught her hand across the softly lit table. "Don't look so distressed, my dear. I shall get over it, be happy enough in my own quiet way. And no doubt in time I shall find the right sort of wife to share the flat with me."

Jennie, clinging to his hand, quoted softly :

"And I shall find another girl,
A better one than you.
And I daresay she will do. . . ."

"Where on earth did you dredge that up from?" John asked with a bitter laugh.

"I don't know. From some poetry anthology, I suppose, and it stuck. I've got that sort of a rag-bag mind. It was an odd little poem, beginning, "Now that we've done our best and worst . . . and parted. . . ."

"Quite!" said John shortly. "Which seems to be our pretty definite cue. Just wait until I've paid the bill and I'll take you home."

It wasn't very easy living through the next few days. But beneath all the awkwardness and unpleasantness of the broken engagement Jennie was conscious of a heady sense of release. She was free! Free as air again. As she walked down the Embankment looking at the raffish row of houseboats anchored in the shallows close to the shore her heart was as light as her footsteps. The muddy old Thames, in full spate after a prolonged spell of rain, managed to sparkle and dance, conveying a sense of life in the wintry sunshine.

Of course there were bad moments: seeing the announcement in *The Times*, cancelling the engagement: 'The marriage arranged etc., etc. will not take place' And there was the trying interview with Lady Davenham, who was half reproachful, half commiserating, understanding Jennie's viewpoint as well as her own and sorry for her inevitable discomfiture. Would nothing ever upset her '*niceness*'? I wish she wasn't quite so good, Jennie thought rebelliously. And John was just like her; kind, patient, understanding. Was that why she hadn't fallen properly in love with him? Was she herself so far from being 'nice' that there had to be a dash of villainy in any man who attracted her?

Glyn Harney!

She must not think of him. Keep the obsession concerning him at bay. For nothing would ever make her believe in his integrity. If he had pleaded with her that evening at the Slavonia it had probably been because in his male conceit he could not endure her angry repudiation of him. And that repudiation still held. Breaking with John made no difference. The whole painful stupid affair of Glyn Harney was irrelevant. She must put it behind her, get on with the business of living.

Though indeed during those first days of her broken engagement she was not quite sure what the business of living entailed. She seemed to be moving in a void. Wherever she turned a vacuum awaited her. No John, no flat in Harley Street to be worried over and worked on; no neatly planned future as Mrs John Davenham. It was all very unsettling, although in so many vital ways a relief, an uneasiness rather than an ache. It was the emptiness left by her father's death which really hurt.

"You must find something to occupy you," her mother advised. "Why not try for a degree in social science or something of the kind?" But Jennie confessed that she was not one of the studying kind, nor did social science appeal to her.

Karla Romaine had taken her daughter's broken romance philosophically, busy once more with her own concerns, and now engaged in the first strenuous phase of starting a new novel. For hours each day she would be shut up in her study, while Jennie wandered aimlessly about the big house, helping Mrs Tracey in a desultory fashion, dusting, or doing the flowers. Sometimes she undertook the household shopping—so unlike the marketing at Zelen. Drifting up and down the aisles of some supermarket she would find herself longing for the cobbled quayside with its colourful market stalls; and she would see again the clear green water in the harbour basin, where the little pleasure boats rocked at anchor. Shutting out the supermarket shelves of mundane goods, she would conjure up the whole vivid scene—a scene she might never see again. The beautiful old houses, the flowering trees, the miniature cathedral perched on its eminence, its twin spires lifted in fragile beauty against the blue sky.

Her father's painting of it had duly arrived in England and was now housed in the vaults of the National Gallery, awaiting a suitable space where it might be exhibited. Mrs Romaine had been notified by the television network concerned that first of the talks on the Romaine painting would be scheduled to coincide with the date the picture was first shown to public.

Meanwhile, it had been seen by the art critics who had written fulsome notices, praising the dead man's genius, and his generosity in presenting this, his last and surely greatest work, to the nation—like Titian, the art critics reminded their readers, who had painted his best work in his declining years. Jennie, reading these notices, remembering the old man's 'Assumption' which she had seen in a church in Venice, painted in his sixties—that great shout of colour, the crimson and gold undimmed by time, an affirmation of unquenchable life. But the soul of a painter never grew old, she thought, and felt the too ready tears pricking behind her eyes. She missed her father more and more as the days went by and wished she could find the occupation her mother had recommended. But what?

One day she decided to clear some of the congestion in her father's studio. Hitherto she had not had the heart to touch his things. The feeling that they were just as he had left them seemed to bring him near. But now as she moved amid the chaos, sorting tubes of paint, brushes in jars, piled-up canvases, it seemed as if he were closer than ever to her, glad of what she was doing. A sentimental fancy, no doubt, but it comforted her, and presently she found herself squeezing blobs of colour in a random fashion on a large palette. Then she picked up a brush and began to experiment, putting the colours on to a sizeable prepared canvas which stood on an easel under the north light of the skylight.

Hours passed in a flash—time ceased to exist. When at last, exhausted, she stood back to survey the result of her efforts she knew that it was amateurish, but there was a hint of promise in it which gave her the urge to press on.

After that she painted every day. She didn't delude herself that she had inherited her father's talent, but she had discovered in herself a need to paint and a great satisfaction in doing it.

Just after Christmas she enrolled at a famous art school and her work absorbed her more and more. Her painting became more disciplined and she enjoyed the companionship of her fellow students, mostly young men and girls about her own age, many of them poor and struggling. Jennie found herself envying them for this. Struggle, she decided, was stimulating. All her life material things had come to her too easily. Having as much money, and more, than you needed could be stifling. But money was not everything. You could be deprived in ways that had nothing to do with financial wealth. It was the emptiness of her own life now which had driven her to painting, forced her to find a satisfaction she might otherwise have missed.

The winter at last went its dreary way and it was April. One evening after a hard day at the art school Jennie had her supper on a trolley in the small sitting room-cum-library which was her favourite haunt. The window by which she sat overlooked the strip of garden which separated the house from the Embankment and the river. Her mother was away, attending a literary conference in Harrogate, so there was no one to talk to but Mrs Tracey, and she, having brought in the supper trolley, had retired to her own sitting room in the basement. To break the silence Jennie turned on the television set and yawned her way through the rehash of an ancient film. When, she wondered, were they going to show the series of talks on Zelen? And would she have to watch Glyn Harney, week after week, conducting them? It certainly wouldn't be shown during the spring or summer. It would be an autumn or winter offering, when the most important programmes were put on.

The old film came to its predictable end and Jennie switched off and opened the window at her side. The trees in the garden and by the river were putting on their shy little new leaves. Sunset clouds drifted high in the sky above the water, and in a privet hedge close to the window a blackbird began to sing. An odd pain stirred in Jennie's heart as she listened to the rapturous flood of liquid notes. Music filled with all the nostalgia of springtime.

"April is the cruellest month" . . . Now who had written that? T. S. Eliot. Only a poet who was sure of himself could have used that clumsy word 'cruellest' so successfully. Finding the volume of his collected works on one of the library shelves, she turned the pages.

Ah, here was the poem she sought. . . .

"April is the cruellest month, breeding
Lilacs out of the dead land, mixing

Memory and desire, stirring
Dull roots with spring rain."

Jennie caught her breath and the ache in her heart was so sharp now as to be almost unendurable. 'Memory and desire', and an endless emptiness. Was that to be her life from now on?

As if in answer to her question the telephone on a nearby occasional table sounded its shrill summons, startling her. Moving from the window, she picked up the receiver.

"Would it be possible for me to speak to Mrs Karla Romaine?" asked a terrifyingly familiar voice.

CHAPTER THIRTEEN

GLYN HARNEY!

Jennie clutched the telephone receiver so tightly that her knuckles hurt. Wildly she glanced at the April green beyond the window, as though she sought a way of escape.

"Is that Chelsea, double four, three four, three two?" demanded the voice at the other end of the line on a note of doubt.

"Who is speaking?" Jennie countered, playing for time.

"Glynn Harney, of the NYZ Television Network," came the crisp response. "Would it be possible for me to speak to Mrs Romaine? It's about a series of talks on the late Mr Adrian Romaine's work which we're planning to include in our programme at a date still to be arranged."

But Jennie hardly heard the explanation for Mr Glyn Harney's phone call, being wholly occupied in trying to pull herself out of the stupid state of shock to which his voice had reduced her. How *could* she react like this after the months in which she had succeeded in reducing him to the merest shadow in the furthest limbo of her waking thoughts? Where now was her pride, her common sense?

"My mother . . . Mrs Romaine," Jennie hastily corrected herself, "is away for a few days." But it was too late to retrieve her disclosure of her identity.

"Jennie!" The name was an exclamation; a cry of urgency in the spring evening. And for a perceptible moment there was a loaded silence, while Jennie, still clutching the receiver, stared distractedly into space. There were no coherent thoughts in her mind—only a strange, instinctive, almost animal panic, something quite mindless and beyond her control.

"If I might see *you* for a few moments, since your mother is not at home," came the voice in her ear, more controlled this time, the urgency muted. "I shan't keep you long. But there are certain questions which have come up in connection with the Zelen talks. Slight changes in the proposed programme which I feel you and your mother ought to know about. I won't keep you long," he urged. "I'm not far away ... if I might just drop in. ..."

She must have acquiesced, Jennie supposed as she hung up the receiver. She certainly hadn't said 'No' to Glyn's request. He was not far away, he had said. She seized the supper trolley with its used dishes and wheeled it hurriedly across the room and out into the hall, to push it through the green baize door which led to the kitchen regions. Then running back to the study she went over to the mirror above the mantelpiece with some vague idea of preparing herself for the ordeal ahead. Though why should she let Glyn's unexpected visit be an ordeal? Hadn't she seen him many times during those last summer days on Zelen without a tremor of her pulses? Days when she had been safely engaged to John and Glyn Harney was no more than a background figure coming and going to her father's studio—a man whose dishonesty she had discovered, and whom she heartily disliked.

And now here she was, gazing feverishly into the mirror, pulling and patting at her hair, as if it mattered how she looked when he arrived. Not that it was a very clear reflection which confronted her, for the mirror was old, a valuable antique, its somewhat murky glass wreathed in floral garlands of golden leaves and flowers. It made her look misty and sad and quite unreal, her reflection wavering, as if seen through watr. Ophelia drowning for love of Hamlet, drifting in immemorial sorrow down her Pre-Raphaelite stream.

When the front door bell sounded she started violently, though she had been expecting it, listening for it. She ran to answer the summons before Mrs Tracey had time to come up from her basement lair.

Glyn Harney, with the April trees behind him, stood on the doorstep. Hatless, tall, a little diffidently, he met her glance. "Good of you to see me," he murmured formally.

"Won't you come in?" she invited with a composure which surprised her. Now that he was here before her in the flesh her foolish tremors had vanished, a strange quietness replacing them. A kind of relief, though she would not acknowledge it as such, as though something she had been longing for had at last happened.

She led the way into the study and seating herself in the armchair by the window, which was still open, motioned Glyn to a couch the other side of the room. It was much too low for his long legs and he looked a little uncomfortable. But she didn't care.

"What was it you wanted to see my mother about?" she enquired tonelessly.

Glyn leaned back on the couch, stretching his arms out along the back of it. Making himself at home, Jennie thought, prepared to criticise his every move. He had lost some of the tan he had acquired on Zelen and looked tired . . . older. But the very blue eyes under their dark brows were clear and direct as ever, deceptively honest. And they were looking at her as if they would search her very soul. It was as if he had not heard her question. But there was only the briefest pause before he answered.

"My programme director has come up with the suggestion that it would be a good idea to have a touch of family background as an introduction to the series on your father's paintings."

"What sort of family background?" Jennie asked.

"That's what we should have to discuss with you and your mother. Pictures of his studio here perhaps, some reminiscences from Mrs Romaine about her life with her husband . . . how they met . . . that sort of thing. And your photogenic self. . . ." He gave her a little bow. "My director is racking his brains to think of some way of working you into the series. After all, your relationship with your father was very close."

Jennie went pink. "The whole thing sounds revolting!" she burst out.

He nodded. "I was rather expecting you to say that. And no doubt your mother will agree with you. But I would have to see her in person, and I'm supposed to use my persuasiveness." He stood up with a shrug. In a moment he would be gone.

"I'm afraid it's been rather a waste of time for you," Jennie remarked politely, "my mother not being here to consider your suggestions."

"When will she be at home again?"

"Next week."

"Perhaps I could phone then to find out when it would be convenient for her to see me?"

So he would be coming to the house again, to use his persuasions on Adrian Romaine's widow—a task he would be well fitted to fulfil. But instead of feeling scornful at the thought she realised that the important thing to her was that he would be here in this house again. Next week. Was there no end to this secret madness which pursued her? Just five minutes in his company and here were her emotions all at sixes and sevens.

She stood up, preparing to see him out. Beyond the open window the blackbird's song soared in its throbbing ecstasy.

"I wonder if, while I'm here, I might have a look at the studio?" Glyn suggested.

"Of course," Jennie conceded, no valid reason for refusing the request occurring to her on the spur of the moment. She walked before him out of the study and led the way up the wide staircase, flight after flight to the attic floor, a journey which seemed to take a long time. She was very conscious of the man close behind her, but neither of them spoke. What was Glyn thinking? Planning? A campaign of cunning which would end in his cameramen climbing these stairs with their cumbersome gear to make cheap nostalgic pictures. Cameramen. A sharp stab assailed her, coming so suddenly that it took her breath away. Once more she was back in the foyer of the Slavonia listening to the brash young voices gloating over Glyn Harney's success with the Romaine girl, conning his way into her father's carefully guarded privacy.

The studio when they reached it was chill and shadowy, the blinds drawn over the two large skylights. Jennie drew one of them back, admitting the cold steady light from the north—a truthful light, presenting only basic reality. No glitter, no gloss.

On an easel in the centre of the room was an unfinished picture of her own, an imaginative abstract study of light coming through a stained glass window to fall in cubes of crimson and purple on to a pale marble floor. It might have been a memory of the little cathedral at Modice. Glyn went straight over to it. "This isn't Adrian's work," he said sharply. "Who did it?"

"I did," Jennie told him.

He swung round to give her a quick intense glance, his dark blue eyes alight. "It's good . . . strong. I didn't know you painted."

"I didn't know myself until a few months ago. I'm working now at St Michael's School of Art. Soon I'm thinking of going over to Paris to put in some time at the Beaux Arts there. I can stay with Claire and Jacques. . . ." Why was she telling him all this? It couldn't matter to him.

They were standing close together, and he had not ceased to gaze down at her, with that strange light in his eyes. "It's the cathedral," he said, momentarily turning back to the painting.

"It might be," Jennie agreed. "It came to me in a kind of dream."

"*Our* cathedral," he said softly. "Do you remember the morning we went there? That golden summer morning when we met in the *place* at the top of the world, with the glory of the sea and the distant mountains at our feet."

"I remember," she said in a small voice, her heart beating so fast that she hardly dared to draw in the long breath which would steady it. And Glyn was facing her again.

"You think I waylaid you that morning, in order to chat you up, as my cameraman no doubt inelegantly put it."

"And didn't you?"

"Do you really believe that, Jennie?"

She forced herself to meet his blazing, impelling gaze. "What am I to believe, then?"

"A story of cross-purposes and crooked answers," he returned enigmatically. "It's true that I recognised you that morning, but not just at first. I saw you standing on the quayside, watching the steamer tie up. You looked so beautiful, so young, so tender and untouched, that my heart ached, as hearts do when perfection is glimpsed in this imperfect world. At that moment there was nothing personal in it. You were a Beethoven symphony, a summer dawn, a nymph carved on a Grecian fresco—the spirit incarnate of the beautiful island which lay before me."

"With Adrian Romaine tucked away somewhere on it." She couldn't resist the spiteful words. She had to go on hating him. The poetic things he was saying to her were ridiculously highflown.

"When *did* you realise just who I was, besides being a Beethoven symphony and a Grecian nymph?" she mocked.

"When we were in the *kafana*, after you'd been hit by that clumsy crane. I'd seen odd press photographs of you and they came back to me. I remembered one in particular, taken with your father in the courtyard of Buckingham Palace when he went to collect some kind of award."

"But you went on pretending you didn't know who I was."

"If I'd told you I recognised you you would have had no more to do with me, vanishing into thin air, never to speak to me again. Once you knew I was a writer and had come to Zelen in search of local colour you would have been on your guard. If I'd told you I was a television writer I would have lost touch with you

183

completely, and that was something I couldn't bear to contemplate."

"Because you were hoping that through me you might reach the elusive Adrian Romaine."

"The thought had occurred to me, naturally. But it was not my predominant thought. That was ... that I mustn't lose you." He moved away from her, his hands thrust into his trouser pockets, his shoulders hunched. "I told you it was a story of cross-purposes."

There was a heavy silence, while she gazed at his disconsolate back, steeling her heart against him. Those hunched shoulders looked so forlorn. He swung round then, his face grimly set.

"I had to go on seeing you, Jennie!" he cried out.

"So you deceived me, deliberately played me along."

His glance implored her. "I didn't deceive your father."

"You didn't tell him about your TV assignment at first," Jennie reminded him.

"I had no intention of including him in that assignment. I must ask you to believe that. When the moment was ripe and my revelation seemed inevitable I did tell him I was connected with the medium. It didn't seem to alarm him. He gave me his confidence and trust."

"He liked you," Jennie agreed, and looking back she remembered how much happiness this man had brought to her father's last days. She put a hand to her heart as if to hold back the flood of feeling that was wakening there. "He was very useful to you in his trustfulness," she said cruelly.

"Yes," he admitted. "He made my expedition to Zelen a great success ... the all-time scoop of my television career," and added after a slight pause, "But that's not quite what it has turned out to be. In fact there are definite snags. It may do me more harm than good in the end.... It's a long story." He glanced round the chaotic studio. "If there was anywhere we could sit, so that I can tell you what happened and is still happening. Perhaps I should explain to you more fully just why I came round here this afternoon."

Mystified, Jennie seated herself in a dusty Windsor chair from which she had to remove a pile of old art magazines. Glyn perched himself on the edge of the dais on which at one time Adrian Romaine's models had posed.

"When I embarked on my series of Mediterranean islands," he began, "and discussed it with my programme director and producer we didn't immediately think of Zelen, the hideout of one of our greatest living painters. That came later, when I'd done the Greek islands. Meanwhile there was an interval during which I was sent to various trouble spots for straight reporting: Cyprus, Vietnam, Ireland. After that Zelen and a possible snoop in the Romaine direction seemed like a holiday. Then I began to read about the island, and became interested in the lyrical descriptions of its beauty, and the history of its struggles to resist invasion throughout the centuries. I found it all very moving. It was in that mood I came to Zelen. Approaching it by sea that June morning I was overwhelmed by its loveliness; the rugged hills, the little bays with their curving white beaches, the town of Modice on its various levels, a poem in architecture crowned by that miniature cathedral. But you know it all by heart, Jennie, even better than I do. I think on that morning I'd forgotten Romaine. He wasn't important at that enchanted moment. Then I saw you...." He made a small defensive gesture, and meeting his vulnerable look Jennie was filled with an emotion that was half rapture, half fear. When he talked like this of Zelen she could not hate him. It was their love for the island which had drawn them to one another.

"I felt I'd come home," he said softly. "That all the puzzles and pains and contradictions of life had somehow been resolved. A moment of destiny."

He stood up and began to pace the floor.

"Well, you know most of it from then on. In the beginning you shared with me the miracle. It was together we walked in the enchanted land. Until I realised that we were not really together because I'd deceived you. I tried to warn you off. . . ."

Jennie's hands were clenched tightly on her lap, and her face was chalk white. "Then I told my father about the stranger who had come to Zelen to write about it, and who admired and loved the cathedral . . . *his* cathedral. He wanted to see you."

"And accepted me more or less on sight; TV background and all in the end. It was just another part of the Zelen miracle that he should want to work with me, and that I should be in a position to give his great painting of the cathedral prominence." He paused for a moment, but she offered no comment.

"When you decided, after hearing an unfortunate conversation between my camera boys, that I was a low-down double-dealer, it hurt, Jennie. But your reaction was understandable. I had deceived you . . . deliberately, since so much, including my friendship with you, was at stake."

"Do you wonder I was angry?" Jennie asked.

He answered her with a look of pain. "You were not the only person who was hurt." He stopped in his pacing and swung round to her. "Will you think I'm cruel if I say I hope our estrangement still hurts? That I may still mean something to you, now that I'm at last in a position to offer you something more than remorse and a plea for your forgiveness."

There was no answer she could give to this; not wholly understanding his drift. She watched him resume his pacing.

"I've kept your father's talks from the clutches of sub-editors," he said, "retaining them to the last letter the way he would have wanted them; Zelen and its gallant history having the predominance, Adrian Romaine the poet-painter merely the instrument recording its past glories. What room could there be in such a series for chatter and gossip? But that, it seems, isn't quite how my bosses see it. They've tried to force me to manipulate the material, introducing popular appeal. This request, for instance, to Mrs Romaine for permission to photograph her husband's studio, asking her to talk of their life together. Using your beauty on the box . . . Adrian's lovely young daughter, the child of his old age to whom he was devoted—and so on and so forth. Gossip column chatter. Just what Adrian wouldn't have wanted. I was nauseated by the whole idea, and if I came round here this evening, ostensibly to relay the suggestions of my superiors, it was because I intended to make my requests in such a way that Mrs Romaine would be bound to refuse them." He gave a wry little shrug. "Harney the double dealer still at his old game!"

He paused then before adding in a low voice, "I hoped too it might give me a glimpse of you, Jennie."

Though the look he turned on her was full of questions she could give him no answers. Words would not come through the churning confusion of her mind. He had spoken of offering her something more than remorse, of begging her forgiveness.

He said, "When I read the notice of your cancelled wedding in *The Times* I had an impulse to write to you saying I was sorry for any unpleasantness you might be going through. But you would only have thought me impertinent. And anyway I wasn't sorry you were free, though it couldn't make any difference to the way things were between us, at the time."

And that's how it still is, she could have told him, but said instead in a toneless voice, "You didn't write to me when my father died. I thought you might have done."

"I didn't dare," he said, and after a moment added surprisingly. "I wrote to Claire and Jacques, with whom, incidentally, I became quite friendly after you left Zelen. Claire, who was angry with me at first, as you know, modified her opinion of me when she realised I was helping her father in his illness. She made me welcome at the villa, and more recently at their home in Paris."

"You've been seeing them in Paris!" Jennie marvelled. "Claire didn't mention it in any of her letters."

"Because it was only last week I was there, being interviewed for my new job. You see, I've been dismissed from my TV post here in London because of my refusal to co-operate over the Zelen programme. I've refused to alter by one syllable the talks as your father recorded them. And though in this I succeeded in forcing my will on the powers-that-be it's the end of my career as a predictable employee. When I've seen your mother next week and made sure she agrees with my attitude about the talks. . . ."

"She *will*," Jennie put in emphatically.

"Fine! Though my failure to get her permission for the proposed changes will be chalked up against me as further evidence of my unsuitability. I shall be more than ever out on my ear . . . dismissed, discredited."

"For my father's sake!" Jennie said. "You've ruined your television career rather than let him down."

"What else could I have done?" Glyn said quietly. "He depended on me, Jennie, trusted me to establish this record he was leaving behind him, and I'm determined to see it through. I've persuaded my bosses to let me return from Paris in October when the talks are due to begin so that I can do the introduction."

"You mean you'll be living in Paris in October?" Jennie queried, not having quite sorted it out about the new job.

He nodded. "I shall be working for Radio Diffusion by then. It's not a very wonderful assignment, but it's a start."

"Then you're finished with television?"

"It looks like it. For the time being at all events."

"And it's all for Adrian's sake." She held out her hand. "How can I thank you, Glyn!"

He took both her hands in his own, drawing her close to him. "Once I sent you away from me, because I had come into your life under false pretences, and that's no foundation upon which to build a true love. Now that I have, perhaps by chance, and because of my respect for your father, made what you might feel to be some small amends I'm asking you to forgive me my deception."

She could not answer him, still trying to come to terms with all that had been said during the last half hour. Glyn loving her, pleading with her. And he had sacrificed so much for her father's sake. Could she not then forget the earlier hint of double-dealing which had bedevilled their relationship? "A story of cross-purposes and crooked answers," he had summed it up.

"True love," she said, searching his eyes for that truth. "Is there such a thing?"

"Could we try to find out?" he asked, and his hands were firm holding her own—as if he would never let her go. "We shall be in Paris at the same time, it seems," he urged.

She did not have to search now for that truth she sought; it blazed in the dark blue eyes looking down at her. "Couldn't we begin again, Jennie darling? Give it a chance. The vision we saw together those early days on Zelen was not a mirage. Nothing will ever make me believe that."

"Oh, Glyn!" was all Jennie could answer. But all her heart was in her voice. And suddenly she was in his arms.

FREE!

Harlequin Romance Catalogue

Here is a wonderful opportunity to read many of the Harlequin Romances you may have missed.

The HARLEQUIN ROMANCE CATALOGUE lists hundreds of titles which possibly are no longer available at your local bookseller. To receive your copy, just fill out the coupon below, mail it to us, and we'll rush your catalogue to you!

Following this page you'll find a sampling of a few of the Harlequin Romances listed in the catalogue. Should you wish to order any of these immediately, kindly check the titles desired and mail with coupon.

To: HARLEQUIN READER SERVICE, Dept. N 306
M.P.O. Box 707, Niagara Falls, N.Y. 14302
Canadian address: Stratford, Ont., Canada

☐ Please send me the free Harlequin Romance Catalogue.

☐ Please send me the titles checked.

I enclose $_____ (No C.O.D.'s), All books are 60c each. To help defray postage and handling cost, please add 25c.

Name _____

Address _____

City/Town _____

State/Prov. _____ Zip_____

Have You Missed Any of These
Harlequin Romances?

All books are 60c. Please use the handy order coupon.
AA

Have You Missed Any of These
Harlequin Romances?

All books are 60c. Please use the handy order coupon.

BB